2 Sides

Part 2

BY UNIQUE WATERFALL

Published by: Unique Waterfall through CreateSpace.com

Edited by: Shades of Soul Productions

Cover design: Daysha Holloway

Email the author: Unique_Waterfall@yahoo.com

Below ISBN refers to print edition:

ISBN-13: 9780988294325

Thank you lord for your strengthen your guidance and your love.....

To the three loves of my life, Day, Dar, Dai you guys are my everything! Know that all that I do or ever done has only been for you all... I love you with all that I am!

To all my supporters thank you for your continued support!

CHAPTER 1

With her hand, still on the mic and her head held high, Nayla stood relieved. As the crowd's roar took her out her trance while still standing on the stage, she couldn't believe it. She had gone through with telling her family, her friends, the whole world that was in this room, that she is a lesbian! Damn, it felt good she thought. Finally, to have it lifted off her shoulders. The burden that she had been carrying around for so long. *What's next, what do I do she thought now that it's all in the open?*

"Let's give it up for Ms. Nayla the Emcee said as she made her way to the stage she just rocked the house!"

As Nayla made her way down the stairs she saw her best friends coming towards her. All with tears streaming down all their faces, Nayla didn't know what to think.

Ming embraced her first then Rachael then Angie. The four friends stood there for what seemed like an eternity. "We love you they all said to her."

"It's going to be ok" said Angie.

"We are so proud of you" chimed in Rachael.

"And we are here for whatever you may need" Ming assured her.

"Thank you" she said as the tears flowed like a stream. "Where are my mom and sister" Nayla asked?

"They're at the table in a state of shock" said Angie.

"We had better get back to them now" urged Ming. The ladies began to walk back to the table all still in disbelief about the way Nayla had just come out. When the four ladies made it back to their seats Nayla's mom and sister was gone!

Nayla didn't know what to think but she knew it would be tough for her mom and sister to hear that she was a lesbian.

"It's ok" remarked Angie.

"Come on, replied Rachael let's go."

As they walked arm and arm Nayla rested her head on Ming's shoulder. "How could they just leave she asked?"

"Don't worry about them or that right now replied Ming let's just get you home." The four friends got in the car and drove to Nayla's house.

Leaving the poetry set everyone was in disbelief, what's next was on everyone's mind. Nayla had rode in the car with her mom and sister so with them leaving so suddenly she was forced to ride back with Ming, Angie, and Rachael.

The ladies all rode in complete silence as it was the longest fifteen minutes of their lives. When Ming pulled up to Nayla's house, everyone expected to see her mom and sister but they weren't there.

Ming held onto Nayla's waist while she opened her front door. Everyone followed Nayla to the living room and sat down. As Nayla continued to cry, Angie went and got some Kleenex from the bathroom while Rachael got Nayla a glass of water. Ming just sat beside Nayla not knowing what to do, say, or feel. She was proud of her friend but sad because of the outcome.

Nayla wiped her eyes and drank a sip of the water. As Rachael and Angie sat down Nayla begin to speak.

"I just want to say thank you guys for coming tonight, it meant the world to me. It had been weighing on my heart and soul what I needed to do. Nayla took a pause; I chose to speak at the poetry set because it was the only way I could face my fears."

"It's ok" Angie intervened;

"No, it's not ok erupted Nayla, I've been running from who I am for a long time and it's time for me to face reality!" Tears started to swell up in Nayla's eyes she dabbed them out with the tissue. "I've known for a long time that I am a lesbian but something happened to me as a teenager that made me lock that part of me away." Nayla begin to tell her friends about her mom catching her and her best friend when she was a teenager.

With tears streaming down her face, "That changed me forever. The pastor, my mom, and everyone praying it out of me! Nayla began yelling, what kinda shit was that?!"

"Because you know what, it didn't fucking work, it only hurt me more! I locked a part of me away, a big part of me and I tried not to let her out but doing that only has me fucked up! I lost a woman who loved me because I was scared to love her back. My first love was taken from me because of what others felt. I just had another woman walk out on me because I was in denial and told her I wasn't a lesbian when in fact I am a damn lesbian! How could it be wrong, how could GOD not love me? He made me this way I didn't ask for this, it was given to me!"

Without saying a word, the ladies got up and embraced Nayla standing in the middle of the living room they embraced while crying for their friend, but at last she was free….

It had been a few weeks since Nayla came out at the poetry set. She was feeling good about facing who she really was and not giving a care about what anyone thought or had to say. She had poured herself into her work not only because of what happened with her family but because of how things had ended with PG. The article that she wrote on PG was being released in a few days and as she picked up the magazine with the photo of her, she stared at it thinking about how she wanted to talk to her. No, she needed to talk to her "Fuck" she thought. Nayla picked up the phone to call PG but she hung up that's not a good idea she said to herself.

"Good-bye," one of her co-workers announced taking Nayla out of her daydream, it was now seven o'clock and she had lost all track of time everyone was leaving to go home. *I guess it's time for me to leave too there's no need to stay.*

"Goodnight everyone," she declared as she left for the evening. Nayla decided she would make a trip to PG's store maybe she could explain herself and her situation. On the drive to the store Nayla thought about what she was going to say to PG, then she began to have all kinds of thoughts run through her mind. *What if she doesn't want to see me, what if she rejects or embarrasses me she mused.* Nayla decided she didn't want to talk to her, it was too soon. Sitting in front of PG's store she didn't get out, hell she couldn't get out! *Damn* was all she could think to herself as she backed up and drove away *maybe another time or another day I just can't do this.*

PG was getting ready to close the store when she saw a car pull up that looked like Nayla's. *Naw that can't be*, PG went to the window to check. "Yes it is, wow she said out loud. Really?" "I wonder what's that all about, why did she come here only to leave" that had PG puzzled?

Not being able to face PG, Nayla pulled off and went home. When she got in she drew herself a hot bubble bath, got in and started to relax. She wished she could go to the spa for a massage. Yeah, I'll call the girls and see if they want to get away for a weekend soon. Nayla got out the tub dried off and oiled her body up. She put on some boy shorts and a tank top. She went to the kitchen to fix herself a plate of fruit and to call Ming. As she walked to her living room to get comfortable, her doorbell rang. *Who in the world* she thought?

"Who is it" she yelled as she walked up to the door?

No one said a word, Nayla then looked through her peephole and couldn't believe it. She leaned her head and put her hands on the door she took a deep breath and then open the door wide.

"Come in" she said as she started to walk away to her living room. "I'm surprised to see you, what are you doing here" she quizzed?

"First thanks for letting me in, I know things ended badly with us. But I saw or I think I saw you come by the store today, was that really you?"

"Yeah, I did, I wanted to talk to you but couldn't, I just didn't know what to say. I wanted to try to explain to you, let you know," Nayla didn't finish she just put her head down.

"Say it" barked PG!

"I came here because I've been thinking about you and wondering if you were ok. I was mad because I was feeling you and then you tell me you're not a lesbian. That fucked me up and pissed me off but then I thought it has to be something."

Nayla interrupted.

"It was something I wasn't being true to myself and what happen between us made me face that. I'm sorry PG I just wasn't in a good space or place in my life."

"Ok so what space are you in now, is it good?" quizzed PG.

"Well yes and no but that's neither here nor there. So, you've been thinking about me?" quoted Nayla as she walked closer to PG. "Let me make it up to you." Nayla put her arms around PG's neck and she whispered in her ear "I'm no longer afraid to be me, I'm out and I'm free!"

Nayla then begin to kiss PG every so passionately.

PG took in Nayla like a breath of fresh air she smelled divine and she wanted to taste her! PG kissed and licked inside of Nayla's ear. Wanting a little more, PG begin to plant kisses all around Nayla's neck, slowly moving down to Nayla's chest

Nayla let out soft moans as PG's tongue made its way down the middle of her chest.

PG lifted Nayla's tank top over her head to expose her perky nipples that were begging to be suckled.

With anticipation for PG to suck on her nipples, Nayla grew extremely wet.

PG's tongue made its way to Nayla's breast, slowly with the tip of her tongue PG made circles around Nayla's full erect nipples. First the left then the right, gently inserting Nayla's full breast into her mouth while caressing and sucking her nipples.

Nayla moaned in pure delight.

After giving Nayla's nipples some brief attention PG's lips made their way down to Nayla's stomach. Kissing and licking her like she was an ice-cream trying to devour every drop.

Tingling from head to toe Nayla was enjoying every touch that PG was putting on her.

Longing to taste her nectar, PG bent down and got on her knees, she moved Nayla's boy shorts to the side so that her tongue could make its way to Nayla's love hole!

With every move that PG made Nayla grew increasingly aroused. Nayla ran her hands through PG's locks, she caressed her hair while PG planted kisses on the lips of her pussy.

"Umm," was the sound that Nayla made.

The sound brought out a rise in PG, now wanting full access to Nayla's playground. PG pulled Nayla's boy shorts down to her ankles so that she could come take them off.

Fully naked standing in her living room PG begins to lick and suck on Nayla's pussy lips her juices danced on PG's tongue like sugar. PG grabbed Nayla's ass while she stuck her tongue in and out her pussy hole, while Nayla rubbed her breast and played with her nipples.

Nayla's legs began to shake as the pleasure that PG was giving her became overwhelming. Up and down, in and out, PG's tongue went savoring all that was Nayla but suddenly PG just stopped!

"What, asked Nayla what's wrong?"

"You know what I don't think this is a good idea," answered PG. She then began to get off her knees and stand up in front of Nayla. Wiping her mouth, "you know maybe we should talk later" declared PG as she backed away from Nayla. "I just stopped by to see if that was really you outside my store. I didn't expect for this to transpire."

Stunned and not knowing what to think, "you're getting ready to leave," choked Nayla?

"Yeah, I should, it's been weeks since we, you know and I don't want to come here out the blue like this to fuck. I'm glad you're doing better and starting to be true to yourself but you have a long journey ahead of you."

"What the fuck! You come here, get me hot and bothered, stick your tongue in my pussy and then you just wanna leave me wet and horny?" bellowed Nayla.

"You and me, remarked PG, Naw I don't think we shouldn't even start that."

"But wait" coaxed Nayla. "What about what happen a few weeks ago?"

"Yeah, I thought you and I could be cool like that, but that's when I thought you were out. You're just coming out and that's an emotional process. I just don't think this you, me, us thing would be a good idea." PG then walked out the living room and out the front door.

"Shit, you could have least let me bust a nut" Nayla yelled to PG as she walked out her house and closed the door.

Nayla was unsure of what to think or make of PG coming and attempting to make love to her but then suddenly leaving. *Really, brooded Nayla, this shit is for the birds. Whatever I'm not going to dwell on PG any longer! If she doesn't want to see me then fine! Hell that chapter ended before it could even begin, you live and you learn time for me to move on.*

PG left Nayla's house not really knowing if she should have or not but she knew that trying to pick up where they left off couldn't happen. *I guess I just needed to hear her tell me what really happen and what was going on.* Feeling tired and drained PG drove home thinking about Nayla and how things ended with her. PG wanted to reach out to her but her pride wouldn't let her. *I got an image to up hold why should I even be giving her any thought? Man, I feel like I'm coming down with something, let me stop at the store to pick up some stuff,* decided PG

When PG made it home she went straight to her bedroom and got her out some jogging pants and a T-shirt from her dresser she then walked to her bathroom and turned on the shower. She didn't feel like standing up so she turned off the shower and let the water run in the tub instead. PG got in the tub of hot water and began to soak. She still had Nayla on her mind as she closed her eyes she had flash backs of tastings her pussy. *Man, maybe I was a little harsh when I left, I really liked her and we could have had a lot of fun. Plus, she has some good ass pussy and I would love to tap that ass again. Maybe I should fuck with her on the low, bring out the lesbian, hell why should I let some other chick get all that good pussy.*

Once out the tub, PG fixed herself some soup because she wasn't feeling too well. "It would be even better if I had someone here to nurse me back to health and fix this damn soup! No stud should be alone and sick, who should I call to come over? she said out loud." PG then begin to look through her phone but the one person that came to mind was Nayla. *Why the fuck am I still thinking about her? Nope not her someone else, anyone else,* she thought!

Once the soup was done PG fixed her a bowl along with her something to drink and she placed her dinner on a tray and went into her bedroom. As she ate her soup she flicked through the channels on the TV. She wasn't in the mood since she really wasn't feeling well. "Damn I need to shake whatever this is I don't have time to be getting sick." PG finished her soup and laid down. As she laid across her bed her mind danced around with all kinds of thoughts and that one person she didn't want to think of anymore. *Things will look up tomorrow, so much to do so little time she deduced.*

The next morning when PG woke up, she still wasn't feeling any better than the night before but she still got dressed and went in to work. At the store, she had some paper work that had to get done and she didn't want to rely on anyone to do that.

"Good morning, everyone" she announced to her employees when she walked into the store.

"Good morning" replied Carla smiling. "How are you?"

"I'm good I'll be in my office if anyone needs me."

"Ok," said Carla, as PG walked to the back of the store to her office.

When PG got to her desk, she picked up the phone to call Nayla. She wanted to apologize for leaving her house the way that she did no need for any hard feelings. As the phone was ringing PG thought about what she would say. She really didn't know what to say and Nayla not answering the phone got her out the hot seat. PG was not one to leave messages so she just hung up the phone.

As PG was hanging up the phone Ray walked into her office.

"Hey man what's up?" Beamed Ray

"Nothing much" replied PG.

"Ooh, you look like shit" said Ray.

"I know, I feel like shit too."

"Maybe you need to go to the doctor and get that checked out" suggested Ray.

"I know man I will call and make an appointment, I just have been so busy and it just came down suddenly."

"I hope so because you look messed up bro, maybe you need to go home and lay down" Ray advised.

"Yeah, I think I will, I'll just have Carla fill out this documentation and I'll go home and rest up."

"That's the best thing you can do, no need of trying to be superman!" Ray teased.

"Shidd, well you know that's my second job" revealed PG laughing.

"In your dreams, now I think it's time for you to wake the hell up" jested Ray!

The two friends walked out of PG's office and to the front of the store.

"Ok man I'll check you later" said Ray as she made her way out the door.

"Ok cool, I'll hit you up maybe this evening once I wake up" PG replied

"Ok dog," and with that Ray was out the door.

PG stopped at the register to advise Carla on all the things she need to have done.

"I'm leaving for the rest of the day because I'm not feeling well. If you need me just call, I'll be at home but I need for you to take care of this for me." PG then instructed Carla on the paper work and what needed to be added.

"Ok PG hope you feel better I will handle everything for you. Take care, see you tomorrow."

"Ok bye" answered PG as she walked out the store and to her car.

When PG made it home, she was glad that she had decided to leave the store early she was feeling much worse and all she wanted to do was just get in the bed and sleep. She knew the store would be in great hands with Carla, and she knew she needed to call the doctor, she just didn't want to hear what they would have to say.

CHAPTER 2

As Rachael drove home from work, she thought what a beautiful day it was. "I would love to get out and enjoy this weather, but I have a busy week ahead so let me just go home to unwind." On the drive home Rachel wondered what DC was up to. It had been a few weeks since their boat encounter and nothing really happen from there, just a few phone calls but no real action. DC had been out the country and Rachael didn't know when she would return. *Ooh, if only I could have gone, I would have love to been on location with her,* thought Rachael. *That isn't possible I have a job plus we haven't gotten close like that yet,* but it wasn't like she wasn't trying.

DC's schedule kept her very busy and Rachael didn't like that she wasn't the center of her attention or affection. *Once she comes back in town, I'm going to make my presence known.* Walking in her front door Rachael called DC, she knew that she would have to leave a message something she's been force to do but usually doesn't. But for DC she will because she wants DC to hear her sexy voice.

When Rachael finally made it home she was exhausted *where is my energy going,* she thought. "I've been so tired lately I need to take a vitamin or something, or maybe I just need a vacation" she said aloud. Rachael turned on a pot of water for some tea and went to the bath room to take a quick shower while the water was boiling. The tooting of the tea pot signaled it was time for her to get out. Wrapped in only a towel Rachael went to the kitchen, made her tea, took her sleeping pill and then walked back to her bedroom. Once in her bedroom Rachael put the cup on her nightstand and laid across her bed. "Whew," she let out a sigh. After a few moments, she sat up to take a sip of her tea, "ooh that's good but it's too hot right now." Sitting the tea back on the nightstand she picked up her remote. She wanted to watch the new movie "The Inside of Out" from Shades of Soul Productions.

******

With DC being overseas on business, it made it hard for her to keep in touch with her friends and family because of the time difference. She knew once she got back to the states she would have a lot of people to see. One person that she was kind of looking forward to seeing was Rachael. Even though DC thought she was such a materialistic person with shallow views, she saw potential in her and wanted to bring it out.

Her and Rachael had been playing voicemail tag ever since she left. DC thought it was kinda cute the way Rachael would call sounding all sexy. They hadn't spent a lot of time together but she knew once she got back to the states she would take Rachael on some very special dates. Show her a simple good time because those hold the best memories. Show her that money isn't everything and there are some things money can't buy.

The sound of the stewardess took DC out of her thoughts. The plane was getting ready to land and in a couple of hours, she would be ready to cut up.

"Please fasten your seat belts" the voice over the intercom commanded "we will be landing momentarily."

Doing as she was instructed DC fasten her seat belt and looked out the window to watch her plane come in for a smooth landing. As the plane made the landing into Midway airport, DC was so happy to be back home. She had decided to buy a condo in Chicago and keep her apartment in New York as well.

"Welcome to Chicago, I hope you enjoyed your flight with MelShore airlines please joins us again soon."

"Thank you lord for a smooth flight" DC professed as she stood up.

"Excuse me," DC heard a voice as she was getting her bag from the overhead compartment. Turning around to see who was speaking to her.

"Yes," answered DC.

"Sorry the voice said but aren't you DC the model?"

"Yes, I am", answered DC.

"Can I trouble you for an autograph please" the voice asked while handing DC a pen and a note pad?

"Sure, who should I make this out to?"

"Mo it's short for Monica, said the voice I look up to you I just came out to my family and being a stud isn't going over to well with them."

"I'm sorry to hear that said DC, hang in there be strong and understand this is your life not theirs."

"Thank you, DC, said Mo, I appreciated that so much."

"You're welcome man said DC as she handed Mo back her pen and note pad."

"Can I ask you a question DC asked?"

"Sure anything"

"How old are you?"

I'm 19, Mo responded.

"Wow, you have so much ahead of you just keep in mind *self-preservation* nothing around you will be happy if you aren't happy. Don't try to live your life the way others want you to. Live your life the way you want." Insisted DC.

"Thanks so much, said Mo as she and DC walked off the plane and into the airport. I can't believe I ran into you. My boys aren't going to believe it, take care and have a great day!" Mo extended her hand to shake DC's.

"No problem, how about we take a picture that way your boys will believe you" DC offered.

"You'll do that for me?" exclaimed Monica!

"Sure," smiled DC.

Mo took out her phone and took a few pictures. "Thank you so much DC you just don't know how much me meeting you like this means to me."

"No, thank you, I appreciated you being a supporter of mine. Don't forget self-preservation, your happiness matters over everyone else" DC said as they parted ways. DC was always humbled whenever a fan young or old approached her. Sometimes they seemed to be afraid but for the most part they would always smile and asked if she was DC the famous model. While walking to retrieve her luggage DC called Kimoni.

"Hey, what's up man" Kimoni said when she answered the phone.

"Nothing much, I just landed I'm getting my luggage now getting ready to leave."

"Sounds good said Kimoni you have a car waiting for you to take you home."

"Cool. Once I get home and settled I'll give you a call."

"Sounds good to me, so you glad to be home" Kimoni asked?

"Hell yeah! I love being abroad but I was so ready to get back to the Chi."

"I just bet remarked Kimoni, your schedule is clear this week so you're free unless something changes just remember to call me once you get settled."

"Ok, said DC will do talk with you later."

"Bye" said Kimoni and the two hung up from one another.

Once DC was in the car she contemplated whether she would call Rachael today or tomorrow. *Maybe I'll surprise her with a little something, something,* contemplated DC. As the driver drove up Lake Shore Drive the sky light of the city at night looked wonderful! DC thought about what she wanted to do for Rachael. DC wanted to show her that she missed her and try to spend a little more quality time with her. The driver pulled up at DC's condominium and opened the door for her. *I can never get used to that, someone else opening my door*, she heeded. That was one of the benefits to being a successful model.

"Hello Ms. Carter" said the door man as he opened the door to the condo. "Welcome back home, how are you today?"

"I'm good Jack, how have things been with you?"

"I'm great Ms. Carter and things are well."

"Sounds good Jack I'll see you upstairs."

"Sure thing" said Jack and out the door he went to get her luggage as DC headed to the elevator up to her condo.

"Whew, finally home" DC said as she opened her door and walked into her place. DC walked into her kitchen and sat her keys down on her counter she then went to the fridge and got her a bottle of water. Just as she was opening the water, her doorbell rang. It was Jack bringing up her luggage and mail.

"Thanks Jack said DC here's a little something for you" DC said as she gave Jack a tip.

"Thanks Ms. Carter let me know if you need anything else."

"Sure thing have a good night" with that DC closed her door.

DC put her mail on the counter next to her keys she didn't feel like looking at any mail she just wanted to unpack, unwind, take a shower and relax from the long flight. It was late and she was ready to feel the comfort of her own bed. "I will call Rachael tomorrow, I just don't have the energy." DC opened her suitcase she didn't even feel like unpacking. She just went into the bathroom and started the shower got undressed and got in.

The hot water felt great on her skin she let the water run all over her face and hair. The warmth of the water had begun to relax her and she couldn't wait to get in her bed. DC lathered up her towel and began to wash up. After washing her body from head to toe, she rinsed the soap off. DC got out the shower and dried herself off in front of the mirror. Once she was done she wrapped the towel around her waist.

She pulled her dreads back and put on a band, "damn it's time for me to get this hair tighten up guess I'll be calling in the morning to set up an appointment." She then applied her facial scrub to her face washed her hands and begin to brush her teeth. After brushing her teeth, DC washed the facial scrub off her face and rinsed her mouth with mouthwash.

DC walked into her bedroom and took a pair of boxers and a tee shirt out her suitcase. "Gotta hit the gym tomorrow I must keep this body tight" she said while looking in her full-size mirror on her bedroom door. DC picked up the remote and turned the TV on she sat in the leather chair that was in her room and put her feet up on the footstool. *It sure would be nice if I had some pussy right now she thought as she folded her arm behind her head. Yes, pussy would be a great thing right now, she pondered to herself.*

CHAPTER 3

The sound of Ming's alarm woke her out of a sound slumber. Slap, she hit the button to stop the noise that was coming out. *Damn is it time to get up already, shit.*

She had been up all night going over a contract for DC to be the face of the new clothing line Stud Ware. Ming would be meeting with the owner of the clothing line Ms. Samantha Banks and her attorney in a few days she wanted to ensure that DC would be getting the best deal possible. Sam was an upcoming clothing designer and she wanted DC and no one else to represent her stud line.

This would be a wonderful opportunity for DC and for Ming's law firm. Kimoni had negotiated a great deal for DC and Ming went over it with a fine toothcomb to ensure that there weren't any legal technicalities of any sorts. Ming went to her kitchen and started her coffee pot she wanted a cup this morning. While her coffee was brewing, Ming jumped in the shower to get started with her day.

As soon as Ming got out the shower and stepped into her room her phone rang.

"Good morning this is Ming."

"Hey Ming, good morning to you too."

"Hey there DC, what's going on, are you back in town?" Ming inquired.

"Yes, my wonderful attorney I was calling to touch base with you to let you know I am back home."

"Ok, glad you're home safe so how was your trip aboard," quizzed Ming?

"It was great but I'm glad to be back home."

"Well we're glad you're back home too, I will have some good news for you in a couple of days revealed Ming. I can't give you any details yet but once I iron everything out I will let you know."

"Sounds good, well let me go yo man, my manager told me I have a couple of free days so I'm getting ready to make the best of them."

Laughing at what DC said, Ming replied, "you do that I'll talk to you later."

"Ok, Ms. La'Ming, bye" and DC hung up the phone.

Still laughing at DC, Ming was getting ready to call her "Man". However, she decided to wait until she got into the office she was already running a little behind and she still had some important things she needed to take care of once she got there.

After hanging up with Ming, DC called True her stylist. True was her nickname her real name is Tameko. True has been DC's hair stylist since she got in Chicago. She was recommended by her former stylist when she moved back home. DC had to admit she was impressed with her work and was glad that she was fortunate enough to have been introduced. True's voice mail came on DC hung up and sent a text instead.

"Hey True its DC I need to get in ASAP my head needs you hit me back."

DC hit the send button and then began to get ready for her day she hoped that True would be able to get her in today that way she wouldn't have to see Rachel with her head a mess. It wasn't all that bad but with her being overseas she wasn't able to get her locs tighten up the way she liked. Just as she wished True hit her back with;

"Hey DC yeah I can get you in today no prob can you be at the shop in an hour?"

"With bells on," replied DC.

"Ok cool see you then" True text back.

DC arrived at the shop right on time. "Hello everybody" she greeted as she walked through the door.

"Hello everyone" replied back.

DC was surprised to see Ray when she walked to the back. "Hey, what's up man" she chimed as she walked towards Ray in the chair.

"Nothing much" Ray replied as she gave DC some dap. "What you doing here?"

"About to get this head taken care of by True asap!"

"Oh ok, I didn't know True did your hair?" Ray said surprised.

"Yeah, since I been back home I've been coming here."

"Well this is the place to be, my fade always be tight this is the only place I will come to get my head done period. Best place on the south side of the Chi," Ray declared.

"Yep, yep," agreed DC.

"I'm ready for you now come on have a seat," True shouted at DC.

"Well I guess that's my que I'll check you out later."

"Aight man I'll see you later" and the two friends bumped shoulders.

"Hey, welcome back home" True greeted DC as she sat down at the shampoo bowl.

"Thanks, it is good to be back."

"So how was your trip," asked True while shampooing DC's hair. "I know it was mad crazy women on top of women go head tell me the juice don't hold back!"

DC started to chuckle "man it wasn't even like that I was over there to work."

"I bet you were working, yeah working them women over and over and over," True teased.

The two then started to laugh.

"No, it was strictly work, plus I have my eye on someone else," DC assured True

"What someone else,I know not the one you told me about a while ago?" asked True while rinsing DC's hair.

"Yeah her" said DC.

"Why are you still wasting your time on that one when it's some many others ones out there?"

"Well it's something special about her and plus I want to show her life isn't all about material shit you know."

"Well good luck with that one cause it's not ever going to go far she sounds like a lifetime user to me but hey I'm always here to listen to them stories you know I lov'em."

"For sure who can I tell if I can't tell my stylist" chuckled DC.

"That's right now come on to my chair so I can get your head right!"

Just as DC was walking to sit in True's chair Ray was done with her hair.

"Hey man I'm outta here but I'll catch up with you later. I think I'm going to go over and check on PG she's been feeling sick."

"Really man imma have to give her a call but tell her I said what's up."

"Ok will do, I'll see you around just hit me on the hip later."

"Aight see ya bro" said DC and out the door walked Ray.

On the way to PG's house Ray called Kim she knew she would get her voice mail but Ray didn't care she loved the way Kim sounded and to hear her baby's voice brought a smile to Ray's face always.

"Hey baby it's me just calling to tell you you're on my mind in such a way that makes me think naughty thoughts. Ok, ok, chuckled Ray let me stop call me when you get a chance."

Ray hung up the phone just as she was pulling up to PG's house. She got out the car and walked up to PG's door she didn't even bother to call because she knew she was on the way she just used her spare key to get in.

"Hey man it's me Ray where you at?" She called out to PG.

"I'm in the bathroom man I'll be right out" PG yelled back.

"Ok I'm going to the kitchen to get me something to drink." Ray walked to the fridge and got a bottle of water. "Hey, man DC is back in town, she told me to tell you hi and that she would be calling you later on sometime."

"Really, asked PG as she walked up to her kitchen where you see D?"

"At "Get U Tight", I went and got the head done today and while I was in the chair in she walked."

"Hell, I didn't know she got her hair done there," said PG.

"Me either, but True was hooking her up."

"Well she's in good hands with True fosho," said PG.

"Man, let me tell you what happen the other day. Tell me why I was closing up the store before I got sick I saw Nayla in the parking lot of the store."

"What! Exclaimed Ray doing what?"

"Nothing man she was just sitting there and then she drove off, at first I thought that can't be her. So, after I closed up I went by her place."

"Tell me you didn't bro, you didn't, did you," asked Ray?

"Yeah I did. I just wanted to know after everything that went down what in the hell she was doing in the parking lot."

"Ok, man spill it, demanded Ray. What happen what did she say?"

"Man she gave me some bullshit about not being in a good place but now she's in a good place. She claims she came to the store to talk but chickened out etc, etc, etc. So through all that talking we started to kiss and then one thing lead to another and next thing I know the panties was coming off and I was going down."

"Man, please tell me you didn't fuck her?"

"No I didn't PG assured Ray, I wanted to but I didn't. She's just coming into her lesbian hood and I don't want to be a part of that, she must find her own way I don't need her trying to lock down on me. You know how new lesbians get when you put it down on them they want to wife you up and shit."

"I know said Ray laughing I know you don't want no repeat of Ronda from back in the day!"

"Hell to the motha fuckin naw! That shit still gives me chills, hell let's not even talk about that no more. I don't need that crazy popping up in my life right now," exclaimed PG.

"I agree I swear never to bring up that shit again declared Ray. So how you feel man she asked PG?"

"Man I'm holding up a little but I still feel sick I have a doctor's appointment in a couple of days so I can find out what's going on."

"Yeah you better or I'll get the crew and we're going to drag your ass. I think you need to go sooner than a couple of days though"

"No need for that man, I'm going to go."

Just as Ray was getting ready to answer PG, she got a text on her phone.

Waiting for you now come and get it....

"Umm, PG something just came up and I gotta run I'll check you out later," she said smiling from ear to ear. "Love you man I'll hit you up later deuces."

"Aight man," later PG then walked Ray out the door.

As Ray made her way to her car she thought, *that's the text I've been waiting for all day.* While driving to her destination, she thought about how she was going to get it and give it too! "Damn I can't wait," she said out loud! As she was pulling up she was being signaled to pull and park in the garage. Following instructions Ray pulled in and parked her car. As she was gathering her things together to get out there was a knock on the window.

"Hey baby what you doing in there, don't you want this?" the woman asked as she took a step back.

Before Ray could answer, the woman opened up her coat to reveal her lingerie outfit.

"Damn baby," as she put her fist in her mouth. "Hell yeah I want that and so much more." Ray then got out the car, took her by the hand, and pulled her in close.

The two-started slowly kissing as Ray began turning her around so that her body was positioned on the car. Ray then began to lick and suck on her neck as if she was hungry for blood. Her skin tasted like strawberries and it tinged all over Ray's tongue. Ray then made her way down to the middle of her chest she planned to expose her breast to the afternoon air. As Ray took her breast in her hand, she admired her nipple standing so perky waiting to be devoured. "Go head baby, they miss you." Ray took her tongue and began to form wet circles slow and sensual she licked her left nipple first then turned her attention to her right nipple as her companion rubbed the top of her head. Ray palm cuffed her breast as if they were made just to sit in her hands. Suckling with nothing but passion Ray gave her nipples all the attention they needed. Taking her hand down to the middle of her body Ray's fingers find their way to her wet paradise. Slowly she slides her fingers inside one by one going deeper and deeper.

"Ooh baby yes!" She moaned throwing her head back while biting her bottom lip as Ray's fingers entered into her.

 In and out her pussy with caution Ray rotated her middle finger as she glided up and down.

She rode Ray's hand as if it was her strap rocking with nothing but pleasure.

Wanting her to feel nothing but ecstasy Ray went faster and faster. Ray's hand was dripping with nothing but juices when she took her fingers out and stuck them in her companion's mouth and whispered in her ear. "Taste your juice baby, it tastes so divine." Ray began to roll her finger on top of her companion's tongue. Suck it baby, suck all your wetness. As she sucked Ray stuck her tongue in her mouth and they begin to kiss fiercely their tongues stroking one another as if they were trying to take each other's breath away.

While still kissing passionately Ray picked her up and sat her on top of the car's hood. She looked up and told her open up your legs wide. Ray then buried her face into her paradise. Licking her clit ever so slowly made her companion let out soft purrs.

"Oh you like that don't you" gurgled Ray as she licked and licked the top of her clit.

"Ooh, Ooh groaned her companion yes baby don't stop please ooh don't stop."

Ray ate her pussy with passion and desire sticking her tongue deep into her pussy hole searching for her G-spot. Want nothing but to please her woman she made love to her like it was their last time. With every stroke, her moaning let Ray know she was doing a good job, no fuck that she was doing a great job! Just as Ray began to do that trick that she does to get to the explosion, her companion's body began to tremble.

"Make me cum baby she called out."

"Daddy going to make you cum in my mouth now give me all your juice Ray demanded."

"Oh baby, I will I will, just make me cum please!"

With the green light, Ray begin to work her tongue magic. Licking and licking with a rhythm that is her signature touch she brought her girl to new heights.

"Baby, baby, her girl began to pant I'm cumin I'm cumin." "OOO OOO, ooohh" was all Ray heard while all in her mouth was the sweet juice that she had worked so hard to get. She swallowed every drop even licking her girl spot once more to ensure she didn't waste none!

Ray begin to plant soft kisses on the inside of her girl's thigh then up her stomach until she reached her mouth. Her girl was panting hard and trying to catch her breath.

"You ok baby asked Ray?"

"Yes, she replied when I told you to come get it I didn't think you would get it like that and right here in the garage."

"Well why not, anytime anyplace don't matter I did what you asked I came and got it," gushed Ray.

They both begin to laugh as Ray got her down from on top of the car. Ray placed her arms around her waist and looked into her eyes and before she planted a soft kiss on her lips, she whispered. "Is there anything else you need for me to do for you my sweet Kimberly?"

"Yes," exclaimed Kim as she backed Ray up to the wall for support and balance. "I need to taste you now." Slowly Kim slide down the front of Ray and got on her knees and started to unbutton her jeans. "Hey what are you doing" Ray asked trying to bring Kim back up. "I'm getting ready to please you just as you just pleased me," Kim responded. Kim then begin to pull Ray's pants down just below her knees followed by print boxers.

"Girl you got me standing out here all exposed" retorted Ray. "Don't be nervous baby trust me I got you" replied Kim. She then began to plant kisses on the top of Ray's package. Bending her head slightly Kim gained access to ray's pussy lips Kim then begin to twirl her tongue in a circle teasing Ray's clit. With every stroke Ray's clit became enlarged making it easier for Kim to take it into her mouth. Passionately Kim sucked on Ray's pussy slowly drawing out her nectar. With every stroke she rolled and sucked harder and faster. Ray's legs begin to tremble as she become more aroused her desire for Kim increased as she looked down at her while she was making her body feel so damn good! Ray ran her fingers through Kim's hair stroking her ever so gently giving her the signal that she was enjoying every moment of this pleasure. Looking up at Ray to see if she was watching turned Kim on even more she rolled her tongue all around Ray's love box and then inserted her tongue into her hole. This made Ray shiver! Feeling Ray's body respond Kim went into over drive, in and out her tongue played in the Ray's hole. After a few minutes of teasing her hole, Kim then began licking and sucking Ray's fat clit trying to bring her to climax. Back and forth Kim's head rocked as she took Ray's pussy in her mouth full throttle. This caused Ray to grab the back of Kim's head and move her in faster and closer not missing a spot, while she took her free hand to hold on to the inside of the door frame to keep her balance. "Umm damn" Ray cooed as her body begins to tingle. "Ooh yes, Kim right there don't stop" Ray commanded as she begin to guide Kim's head faster and faster! "Ooh shit ooh shit" was all Ray could utter right before she exploded and gave Kim the juice she was working so hard to get!

"Damn baby your head game is fi!" Ray praised Kim

Kim stood up and gave Ray a big kiss, after breaking free "now come on in the house she said cause if anyone was walking by I know they heard us."

Ray started to laugh and replied, "good, then they know what giving good head sounds like." The two then left out of Kim's garage and went into her house.

"Whew, you just took all my energy I thought I was going to work you over," Ray said as she closed the interior door that led to the garage.

"Nope, you almost did but I gave you a taste of your own medicine" they both begin to laugh.

Once inside the ladies made their way to the bathroom. Kim got in the shower while Ray stood at the sink and washed her face and hands.

"Oh, you going to wash me off of you," joked Kim.

"No baby you're always all over me and in me I could never wash you off!"

"That's what I like to hear said Kim as she lathered up and begin to wash up. Hey you should be in here with me she teased"

"I'm two steps ahead of you" said Ray as she removed her clothing and got in the shower. The two ladies lathered up their towels and begin to wash each other up. They enjoyed each other body even more under the warm shower water. After a little bit more of shower play Ray washed up one last time, rinsed off and exited the shower. She pulled a towel down from the towel rack, picked up her clothes she had placed on the sink and walked into Kim's bedroom. Ray picked up the remote and flicked through the channels on the TV. "It's not shit on," she thought to herself "nothing." Just as she was getting ready to put the remote down in walked Kim.

"You miss me Kim teased?"

"Of course, I did baby, now come lie down on the bed and let me lotion up your body for you" commanded Ray.

Kim surrendered to Ray's command and walked over to the lounge chair where she was sitting. Kim gave the lotion that was in her hand to Ray and then proceeded to lie back on the bed.

Ray touched and caressed every inch of Kim's body with the lotion.

"What would you like for lunch," asked Kim?

"Doesn't matter, I'm all done baby."

"Thank you, my love, you are so attentive to me and I appreciate you greatly," replied Kim.

"You're welcome baby, anything I can do to show you what you mean to me I'll do," beamed Ray as she leaned and kissed Kim softly on the lips. After sharing a long and passionate kiss Kim walked into the kitchen followed by Ray.

"Yeah, I am famished so cook me a meal woman," Ray joked.

"You just ate me all up and now you're hungry," replied Kim with a sly smirk. *Umm OK, what can I fix,* thought Kim as she opened her refrigerator door then the freezer. "How about some turkey burgers she asked?"

"Sounds good said Ray you get them started and I'll finish them off."

"You're that hungry," Kim asked?

"Yes baby, you know our sessions give me a major appetite."

Laughing and shaking her head Kim begin to prepare their food. *Man I'm so lucky, who would have thought running into Ray that afternoon would have led to this. Something so special, me happy, and in the beginning of a new relationship!* "Thank you, God this has been long overdue and I've deserved it even longer," she whispered to herself.

CHAPTER 4

"All done, you like this," asked True as she turned her chair around and handed DC a mirror so that she could check out her hair.

"Man, on point as always, it's no need to even ask. Girl, I sure do miss you when I 'm on location. I wish I could take you with me cause those other stylists don't have nothing on you."

"Why thank you, I do try. I'm here to make you look good but you don't need much help with that with your fine ass."

"Blushing thank you, you are a pleasure on the eyes too!"

"Well I could pleasure more than your eyes," True said under her breath.

"What did you just say" asked DC, looking kinda puzzled. *I know she just didn't say what I think she said*, DC thought.

"Oh nothing, I was just thinking about something don't pay me any attention. Thanks for the compliment and when you're ready to taste this ooo, I mean I'm sorry. I meant when do you think you will be ready to try that new color? Maybe in two weeks?"

"You tell me when the best time to try it and I'll be ready. DC stood up and went into her pocket and pulled out her money to pay True. Here you are for your wonderful services thanks again DC said as she handed her the money. DC walked to the front of the salon, have a great evening everyone take care," and DC walked out the salon door.

As DC walked to her car she tried to wrap her mind around what had just happened in the salon. "Was True? Naw, not True, I'm going to leave that alone." DC phone rang as she opened her car door it was Kimoni.

"Hey Kimoni, what's the business?"

"Nothing much my man, just checking in on you to see what you were doing on your rare free day."

"I just came back from getting the hair done why what's going on, you got something you wanna get into?"

"Naw, nothing in particular but how bout you stop by and we can talk business," Kimoni said.

"Ok give me about an hour and I'll be there."

"See you then," said Kimoni and the two hung up.

DC decided to stop and get something to eat and take it with, she was in the mood for some Thai and she knew a great place to stop. DC called ahead so that she didn't have to wait. After picking up the food DC headed straight to Kimoni's place she was hungry and anxious to eat. DC was surprised when she walked into Kimoni's building that the doorman wasn't there, "strange" she thought. She just signed in and went straight to the elevator.

Man, this day sure got away from me, I wanted to call Rachael. Maybe later tonight so we can get together tomorrow, DC considered. When elevator stopped on Kimoni's floor off she got and made it down the hall to her friend's apartment. DC knocked on the door and after a few moments it opened.

"Hey man come on in I was just getting ready to fix something to eat."

"Don't bother bellowed DC as she raised the bag that was in her hand, I have Thai!"

"Oh yeah! That's right on time, get yo ass in here I'm starving," declared Kimoni.

DC walked into Kimoni's place as Kimoni closed the door behind her.

"Man, I'm so glad you stopped I sure didn't feel like fixing shit." Kimoni walked over to her kitchen cabinet and got down two plates. "Please tell me you got pot stickers she asked?"

"You know I did, right here for ya," said DC.

"Well pass them bad boys over to me my mouth is watering. So how was your trip Kimoni asked?"

"It was cool I was just home sick and ready to get back to my own bed," expressed DC.

"I so understand let me just say thanks for this food it's great," professed Kimoni. The two then begin to discuss in length DC's foreign trip into the wee hours of the morning.

******

Rachael had called and left DC several messages to no avail, she thought DC had made it back home or at the least was on her way back to the states. At any rate, no matter what the case she could have at least called her *damn,* thought Rachael. *I'm not going to keep chasing her ass, it's too many damn RL's out here for me to continue to focus on one that is clearly not focusing on me. Let me just get into my office and start my day and forget about all else. Maybe I'll call Ming to see if she heard from her, naw Ming is so damn uppity that she wouldn't breach her clients' confidential whereabouts. Damn what to do what to do, ok I'll give DC one last call and the outcome of that will determine what I do next.*

Rachael then pulled into the parking lot of her job and went inside.

"Good morning Marie," Rachael greeted the front desk clerk as she walked passed to her office.

"Good morning Ms. Wilson," replied Maria as she was checking a guest out of the hotel.

Rachel picked up the phone as soon as she got in her office. She called Ming's law office she was going to try to pick her for as much information as she could without being obvious.

"Law offices of La'Ming Foster, Angie speaking how can I assist you?"

"Hey Angie, good morning girl it's me Rachael is Ming in yet?"

"Nope not yet, she will be in a little later she worked late last night doing some work for your woMan I think."

"Oh really, do you know what she was working on," inquired Rachael?

"No I don't miss nosey, and if I did I couldn't tell you, why don't you find out from DC yourself?"

"If I could I would, I haven't heard from her," sighed Rachael.

Just as Rachael was about to finish a text came through on her cell phone. Picking up her phone to see who was texting her.

Hi Rachael its DC I'm home and I would like to see you this evening if that's possible? I know

it's early but I wanted to make sure you're
available. Text me and let me know.

"Oh shit girl! DC is texting me now let me go I'll talk with you later," she exclaimed to Angie. Rachael hung up her office phone and begin to text DC, she didn't want to seem too anxious even though she was but she couldn't lose her cool.

"Good morning DC, welcome back home and yes
I will be able to see you this evening around
what time?"

"Can you meet me at on the corner of Randolph
and Columbus at 7:00?" DC asked.

"Yes I can see you then," replied Rachael.

"Ok see you tonight," DC texted back.

Umm, I wonder Rachael assess. Ooh I can't wait it's been forever and we still really haven't gotten a chance to be cozy. But tonight, maybe be different and if it takes giving a little bit then hell that's just what I'm going to do. Rachael began her day feeling great nothing was going to get her in a bad mood. For tonight she had a date with DC and she was ecstatic!

"Let me hurry up and get my work done today, I'm going to leave a little early so that I can go home and freshen up a bit before I meet with DC this evening."

Rachael hurried along with her daily routine not taking any chances she wanted to look and smell perfect for her date with DC. *Tonight, I'm going to make her mine and she won't ever want to go a day without talking or seeing me. Let's get it,* she thought to herself.

******

DC was happy that Rachael had agreed to meet up with her later on this evening. She had a wonderful night planned, something she hoped Rachael would like and certainly appreciate. *I need to get things ready and have her gift for tonight wrapped,* DC expressed. She then got up, got dressed, and took off to the mall. *If I get to the mall early I will beat the crowds, that's the plan,* she told herself.

On the way driving DC called Kimoni she needed her to take care of something important for tonight. After she was done giving Kimoni all the details and how she wanted things done DC pulled into the parking lot of the mall.

"One thing down, just a few more to go!" DC dropped off the gift to be wrapped and headed into the music store. "Let me see if I can find some me some music in here." While browsing DC saw a lot of old school music that reminded her of her child hood. It made her laugh out loud and say, "man I haven't heard this in years, I think I'm going to purchase this."

Upon exiting the store DC ran into Stony.

"Hey there man," she said to Stony as they gave each other some dap and a hug.

"What cha doing here in the mall," Stony inquired?

"Running a few errands, I had to drop off something to get wrapped for a date tonight and then I stopped in this store to browse through the music section to see what they had." "What you doing here," she asked?

"I came in here to pick up some cologne and some other stuff I needed." "I might pick up some artwork, it's a chick on the other side that has some helleva art," replied Stony.

"Shit I just may have to check that out myself, hey I'll check you out later man let me go and see some of this art work."

"Aight man," said Stony. 'Check you out later," the two friends parted ways.

DC walked to the other side of the mall to check out the art that Stony had just told her about. When she got to the table she was blown away. The artwork was spectacular after some negotiating with the artist DC ended up purchasing a couple of the artist's works. Her favorite was a piece called "Lesbian Love" it was beautiful. It featured two women laying on a chaise lounge. One woman was lying on top in between the other women's legs straddling her in a very sensual manner. It was very erotic. After her portraits were wrapped DC made her way to pick up the gift she had wrapped earlier. She then made her way back home to get ready for her evening with Rachael.

Once she made it home DC texted Kimoni to make sure everything she asked for was in place. After getting the everything is all cool, and ready reply DC laid on her lounge chair and relaxed until it was time to get ready to leave.

***** *

Rachael was excitedly looking forward to what DC had in store for them this evening. She was so ecstatic to be meeting up with her but she didn't want her enthusiasm to show. She needed to stay cool and play her cards just right. Time was winding down and her anticipation was growing. Finishing up with all her paper work and signing off on the product inventory Rachael called it a day. Rachael left work with pep in her step she needed to get home, freshen up and be ready for whatever DC had planned.

Looking at her watch it was almost time to meet DC, Rachael thought about being a little late like she always did when she met one of her RL's, but she decided against it. She hadn't seen DC in a while and she couldn't wait to see her. Checking her face and her tits one last time as she passed the mirror, *perfect* she thought to herself as she walked out the door and to her car.

Rachael didn't see DC's car as she pulled up, the time on her car radio read 7:00 p.m. on time with about a moment to spare. As she parked her car Rachael could see DC walking towards her. *Damn umm, I wonder what she feels like.* DC tapping on her window brought her out of the daydream and put an enormous smile on her face.

"Well hello there beautiful," DC said as Rachael opened her car door.

"Hello there handsome," Rachael replied.

DC took Rachael's hand and helped her out the car, as Rachael stood up DC pulled her in close and planted a wet and sensual kiss on her lips that took Rachael's breath away.

"Did you miss me?" "Your lips certainly say you did." DC asked when the two-finished kissing.

Smiling Rachael replied, "I think yours just told me the same thing."

The two ladies laughed. "Come on my sweet, let's get going my car is right over there" DC instructed.

"Oh, we have to drive, I thought we were going to be in the area," inquired Rachael?"

"No, we have to drive it's only a few blocks from here," replied DC as she opened the passenger side door of her car and helped Rachael in. "That's not a problem is it?" "You're not scared to be alone with me," DC teased.

"No not at all but you may need to be scared to be alone with me Rachael," teased back.

"Challenge, I like that, maybe we will see later," DC said as she started the car and took off.

"Ok my lady we're here," DC announced as she parked and turned off the car.

Looking out the window Rachael wondered what and where in the world they were, there wasn't nothing but a park insight. "Where are we," Rachael turned and asked?

"You'll see in just a moment, but right now I need to blindfold you so you can't see what I have in store. Turn back around and let me put the blind fold on you," DC commanded.

Doing as DC instructed Rachael turned around and allowed DC to place the blindfold over her eyes.

"Now sit right there beautiful and let me guide you on this magical ride." Getting out the car DC went to the trunk to retrieve Rachael's gift. Proceeding to the passenger side DC opened the door for Rachael. "Are you ready my lady, give me your hand?" DC helped Rachael out the car and guides her through the park and into an exquisite enclosed wrap around garden.

It was decorated with candles a small dance floor a larger projector screen with soft music playing in the background. The food table was a buffet of all kinds of fruits and veggies. The aroma coming from the warmers set off a delightful scent to their noses.

"Just a little further," DC instructed Rachael, DC directed Rachael to a bench and helped her sit down. "Ok we are here but before I take the blindfold off let me say thank you for allowing me to guide you here and I hope you enjoy our evening tonight."

When DC took the blindfold off Rachael couldn't believe her eyes! She was in a beautifully enchanted garden filled with all types of flowers and food.

"Oh my goodness, this is awesome! Ooh just simply beautiful thank you for bringing me here!" Rachael stood up and gave DC a long passionate kiss.

"You're welcome said DC I hope you like it."

"I do, oh my it's so nice, this is something so different wow just lovely!" Rachael professed.

"Well look around, smell the flowers we will be here for a moment, unless there is somewhere else you have to be," DC quizzed?

"Not at all chimed Rachael I'm right where I want to be." Rachael couldn't believe her eyes she had never experienced a Garden of Eden such as this one. This isn't where she thought her and DC would be on their date. As Rachael was walking around the garden DC came up behind her with a glass of wine.

"Here you go beautiful, let's toast, to having you here with me tonight and me being back home to enjoy your company."

"Cheers" the two ladies clicked their glasses.

"Well what do you think," DC asked Rachael?

"It's all so beautiful, thank you so much, I can't believe my eyes, and that you did this all for me?" Rachael exclaimed!

"You're welcome responded DC, I wanted to do something special and intimate to show you my romantic bone."

"Well you did and this is great," beamed Rachael.

The two ladies then took a sip of their wine.

"Well my lady shall we have a look at what we will be dining on, are you hungry?" DC asked as she lead Rachael to the table with the food.

"Famished," Rachael says with a smile.

"Well we have all this to choose from," DC lifted the lids off the warmers to reveal what was teasing their noses with that wonderful aroma.

"It all looks so good I don't know what to try first, my eyes maybe bigger than my stomach."

"No worries mine two, but none the less let's eat." Professed DC.

The two ladies begin to fix their plates once they were done they walked over to the table to sit down.

"Just one moment DC told Rachael let me put my plate down." DC sat her plate on the table and walked over to Rachael and pulled out her chair.

"Thank you so much," Rachael replied.

"You're quite welcome," DC said with a smile.

Sitting down in her own chair DC took Rachael hands in hers and said, "would you do the honors of saying grace?"

Suddenly put on the spot Rachael didn't know what to say or do. She had never had to say grace other than just saying God bless this food. Rachael was at a loss for words.

"Ummm I don't know what to say," she told DC embarrassed.

"Well just say what's in your heart right now and it will be ok."

"Ok," Rachael responded as she grasps DC hands firmly, she took a deep breath cleared her throat bowed her head and closed her eyes.

"Thank you lord for this wonderful night that we are having and I pray that DC and I have many more Amen."

Shocked and stunned! "Amen," DC repeated. "You're done she asked?"

"Yes, I am," Rachael contended.

"Well let me add to that," and DC begin to pray.

"Father God we humble ourselves before you and ask that you bless the food that we are going to receive for the nutriment of our bodies. Bless those who prepared this wonderful meal and bless those who are less fortunate in your name I pray Amen"

"Amen," Rachael chimed in softly.

DC picked up her fork, "let's eat," she said as she put some food up to her mouth. Stunned by Rachael's blessing DC didn't know what to say. She wasn't going to present her with the present she had for her, *not now, damn she can't be this fucking shallow, please not another one,* she thought to herself. Rachael asking her a question interrupted her thoughts.

"So how have you been and how was your trip" Rachael inquired?

"It was good, I was just ready to come back to the states and how are things for you," DC asked?

"I'm good just busy at work," Rachael said as she took a bite of her food. "I'm glad things went well for you."

"Me to," replied DC. "Me too."

The ladies continued eating but the evening became quite awkward. DC didn't want to deal with another self-centered shallow chick she had seen enough of them in the business.

Sensing the tension Rachael didn't know what happened, but she didn't want things to get any worse so she made up an excuse to end the date.

"Oh, DC it's getting late she said and I have an early conference call in the morning. Do you mind if we call it a night?"

"Oh no, sure," answered DC.

"I'm so sorry, I should have told you in the beginning," Rachael tried to explain.

Cutting her off, "it's no problem, let me just make a phone call and I'll take you back to your car." DC then got up from the table and walked away.

"Ok are you ready to go?" DC quizzed upon her return to the table.

"Yes, and I'm quite sorry about this maybe we can go out again sometime" Rachael asked?

Taking Rachael hand to help her up from the table DC answered, "maybe so let's just play it by ear."

The two ladies walked back to DC's car. Once at her car DC helped Rachael in.

"Oh, give me a sec I'll be right back," DC informed Rachael.

DC went back to retrieve the gift that she had. She certainly wasn't going to give it to Rachael right now so she just put it back in the truck of her car.

"Ok you ready?" DC asked once she got in the driver's seat. "Fasten your seat belt and let's ride," she remarked. The ladies made small talk until they arrived back to Rachael's parked car.

"Ok let me get that door for you my lady," DC told Rachael.

Once out the car DC walked Rachael back to hers.

"Thanks for the evening it was great," Rachael announced as she hit the lock for her car door on her key ring.

"You're welcome, I'll give you a call sometime this week."

"I look forward to it," replied Rachael as she started the engine.

"Drive safe and talk to you soon," DC retorted.

"You too and I'll talk to you later," asserted Rachael.

When Rachael drove away she tried to go over in her head what went wrong? *The date was going well, until we started to eat she thought, I wonder why?*

As DC watched Rachael drive away she couldn't help but wonder what she could do to help Rachael see the meaning of life and not the price of it.

"Hey you," a voice called out. "What are you doing just standing here looking crazy," the voice asked?

The question took DC out her trance and when she looked up it was True walking towards her.

"Hey True, what you doing walking" DC inquired?

"Umm, I have to walk to get to where I'm going," True joked. The two ladies started to laugh.

"I know that, I was just saying, oh never mind. How about where are you walking to?"

"Up the street to catch the train," True answered.

"No you're not," DC objected. "Come on get in I'll take you where you need to go." Opening the passenger side of the car door, so that True could get in.

"That's cool with me True agreed, thanks a million."

DC closed the door and hopped in the driver's seat.

"Ok my fabulous hair dresser, where to?"

"Bronzeville please, 45th and Prairie" True stated as she was texting on her phone. Looking up from her phone, "hey what were you doing down here," True inquired?

"You don't even want to know, I just had a date with Rachael you know the lady I've been telling you about."

"Where is Miss, I am the universe" True snickered in a joking manner.

"Ha ha you got nothing but jokes, well it didn't, naw I shouldn't say it didn't. She just, well let's just say she needs to work on some things," DC revealed.

"Well whatever she needs to work on I hope she does, I really do" stated True.

"Can I ask you a question True?"

"Sure, what is it," True smiled?

"Are you busy, do you mind coming with me real quick?" uttered DC

"Come with you where blurted" True?

"I want to go give out something just say you'll go with me," DC begged.

"Ok, ok, you got me in the car already so yeah I'll go," laughed True.

"Thanks, I'll explain it all to you on the way."

When DC and True arrived back at the park True couldn't believe her eyes.

"Wow! DC this is beautiful and you did all this?"

"Well not technically, I told my manager what I wanted and she took care of it."

"Well damn, you are certainly romantic, it's lovely. So where is the stuff you need my help with?" Marveled True.

"Right here True," as DC instructed True to come to the table.

The two ladies packed and organized all the items.

"Whew, ok now all we have to do is load this up in my car," uttered DC.

"Well what about all that other stuff there," asked True pointing to another table?

"Someone else will be handling that," disclosed DC. "We just need to take this stuff right here."

"Ok then, let's get to it," True commanded as she picked up a handful of containers.

"Ok captain, I'm right behind you," DC teased.

While walking up to her car DC popped her trunk and unlocked the doors. "Ok let me place these inside the car and you put the ones you have in the trunk."

Doing as she was instructed True went to place the containers in the trunk of DC's car. *What beautiful wrapping paper,* she thought to herself.

"Are they fitting ok back there?" DC hollered from the back of her car to True.

"But of course, I can make anything fit anywhere" True said jokily.

"Girl you are something else," DC said as she walked to the back of her car to close the trunk. "Come on get in so we can get going." DC walked to the passenger side and opened the door for True.

"Thank thee," True nodded.

DC just chuckled as she got in and started the car. "Alright we're off," she said as she drove towards downtown.

As they were driving True turned to DC and declared. "I think you are such a special person inside and out and I am glad you asked me to accompany you to pass out this food to the homeless."

"No thank you for agreeing to come with me," DC said blushing. "Because not everyone would."

The two ladies then just rode in silence not uttering a word but just listening to the radio.

CHAPTER 5

It had been a few days and PG was only feeling slightly better. "Come on let me get up," she tried to convince herself. "I have shit to do and a business to run!"

Gathering all of her strength PG got up out of bed and took a shower. Once she was done, out the door and to her store she went. It was very early when she arrived and no one was there yet. That's the way she wanted it, she had been off a few days and she just wanted to check and see how well her manager had taken charge. As PG made her rounds through the store, everything seemed to be in order. When she was done with her visual check PG went to her office. She sat down at her desk and turned on the computer to check through the store's inventory and do some software updating that was long overdue.

PG was so engulfed with her work she didn't hear Carla walk into the office.

"Good Morning Ms. Glover," Carla greeted. "I didn't know you were coming in today."

"Good morning Carla, yes I have to try and shake this off. Can't let it get me down, how were things while I was out," asked PG?

"Things were fine, no problems arose. We received that new shipment of jeans, but I'm zoning the store to get the display up today," answered Carla.

"Good, good thank you Carla for all your hard work. I will be in my office doing payroll and checking over some paper work if you need me."

"Ok Ms. Glover good to have you back," Carla responded before she left out of the office and closed the door.

PG turned on the radio she wanted to listen to some music while she did her paper work. The day was flying by and PG couldn't be happier, she was ready to go home and get some rest. *Only a couple of hours left*, she anticipated.

Stony had decided to stop by Frames she wanted to check up on PG and pick up a Tee-shirt and a cap while she was there.

"Welcome to Frames," the clerk greeted Stony when she walked into the store.

"Thanks sweetie, is your boss here today," Stony asked the clerk?

"Yes, she's here would you like for me to go and get her for you," the clerk responded back?

"No that won't be necessary I'll just go into her office but thanks," Stony said as she made her way to the back. When she got to PG's office door it was closed so she knocked softly.

"Come in," PG commanded.

"What up Boi," Stony greeted PG as she walked in. "How are you doing I heard you were sick?"

"Yeah man, I'm better now," explained PG. "I just had a bug or something but I'm good. How are you?"

"Can't complain living, loving, learning, you know my motto," professed Stony.

"I hear that, hey how you know I was sick," inquired PG? "Ray called you or something?"

"Naw, I ran into DC at the mall and she told me I guess Ray told her. But I came to check you out, I thought you would be at home resting. Then I remembered you're a workaholic like me."

They both started to laugh.

"You know me all too well, I have to keep going I was at home for a few days but I needed to set foot in my baby and do payroll."

"Ok, well have you been eating? Knowing you the answer is going to be no," chided Stony.

"You're right, I haven't had much of an appetite," PG admitted. "I had a taste for some soup but just not in the can something home made you know."

"What time you leaving the store today," Stony asked PG?

"Not sure maybe by five why what's up,"

"I'll make you some soup and bring it by the house later on," said Stony.

"Don't play you know I love your soup what kind are you going to make," PG begged?

"Whatever kind you like just tell me and you got it."

"Chicken noodle and a big pot," PG used her hands to animate big.

"Ok big it will be, let me go so I can get started. It's a Tee shirt and cap I want before I leave, so I'm going to get outta your hair and shop for a minute." Stony then made her way out of PG's office.

"Cool I'll see you later tonight." After Stony left out the office PG called up to the front.

"Hey Carla, whatever my friend gets after she pays just comp it and just bring the money to me." PG couldn't wait to get home and taste some of Stony umm umm soup!

When Stony left the store, and got to her car she called Ray, but it went to voice mail. Stony ended up leaving a message.

"Hey Ray it's me Stony call me ASAP!"

Stony was concerned about PG yeah, she sounded fine but she looked a little green. That bullshit about she was ok and she just had a bug wasn't sitting well. PG looked sicker than she was trying to let on. Stony decided not to cook the soup at work but to do it at home. She went into the office to check on her staff and to make sure everything was ok before she took the day off.

Upon arriving at work the kitchen was getting a delivery. Stony went into her office to let her assistant Lynn know, she wouldn't be working today, but if they needed anything to call and she would be back in to help.

"Oh that's fine, you need a day off anyway it's long overdue," insisted Lynn.

"Thanks Lynn, see you guys tomorrow." Off Stony went out the door to head to the grocery store to pick up the ingredients for the soup.

Stony had stopped at a coffee shop that was on the way to the grocery, she wanted to get a cup of green tea.

As Stony walked in looking down at her phone, Angie was walking out. Angie had her head down fumbling through her purse and the two ladies nearly collided.

"Oh excused me I'm so sorry," Angie was apologetic.

"No excuse me" Stony replied I wasn't paying attention."

"Me either, I was just looking for my car keys added Angie. I should have had them in my hand hun, Stony is that you," Angie asked taking another look?

"Yes, it is me." answered Stony. "Hello Miss Angie, how are you?"

"I'm fine sunshine, sorry about almost knocking you down have a great day," and out the door Angie went.

"You to," stony called out as Angie made her way out the door. *Umm, she didn't come on to me not once, very interesting.* A puzzled Stony made her way to the counter to order her tea.

"I'm so proud of myself Angie thought, I didn't hit on Stony and I keep it moving. This new path I'm on being less aggressive and more passive is intriguing. It was so hard for me not to flirt but, I know in the end changing this behavior is for the better."

Angie's lunch break was over and back into the office she walked. Once she got back to her desk and sat down she called Ming to let her know she was back.

"Come into my office Ming instructed, I need for to do something."

"Yes ma'am, what can I do for you," Angie asked?

"I need for you to look into booking me a flight out of town. Looking at my schedule it maybe in a couple of days, so see what you can find for me. I also am going to need a room, so once I'm done with this conference call we can talk more details. But in the meantime, let's look for something in about a week." Ming handed Angie a piece of paper with the out of town information.

"Will do, anything else you need?"

"No, not at this time," Ming replied.

Angie then left out of Ming's office to start her search for flights and hotels.

After doing some extensive searching Angie found what she was looking for and buzzed Ming's phone. "Hey, I found a great flight and hotel accommodation she informed Ming. Would the next 4 days be ok for you to leave or is that too soon?"

"No that's perfect, go ahead and book it, the sooner the better. Thanks Angie!"

Doing as instructed Angie booked the hotel and air fare for Ming's business trip. Once she was done Angie searched for flights to New York she had some vacation time saved and she wanted to take a trip. *New York, New York, yep that's where I'll go!*

Angie picked up the phone to call Rachael, she wanted to know I what happen with DC.

"What's up Angie," Rachael said dry as hell.

"What's Up" What's wrong with you, are you mad or something?

"No, Yeah, I guess exclaimed Rachael. I'm kinda feeling funky about my date with DC. It didn't go all that well."

"What happened girl tell me," chimed Angie.

"Nothing in particular, it's just things seemed ok and then they went downhill."

"Downhill how exactly, what did you do explain yourself," said Angie.

"Well things were cool until she asked me to say grace."

"Ok, well what did you say," demanded Angie!

"I just said "thank you Lord for this date and I hope DC and I have many more" boasted Rachael.

"That's all really Rachael, and you're serious?" Angie asked.

"Yeah why, what's wrong," Rachael asked confused?

"What's wrong with it! Hell, what's right with it," exclaimed Angie. "You didn't even bless the food seriously you need to get your life together! No wonder things turned sour," Angie laughed.

"Whatever, DC didn't mind," Rachael crowed.

"Yeah keep thinking that, your lack of saying grace shows just how vain your ass is," contended Angie.

"Yeah, yeah, yeah, I guess like I said DC didn't have a problem, so what you're talking about doesn't matter."

"Ok Rachael I'm going to say it again, keep on thinking that, but rest assured you heard me say it first" Angie avowed. "Don't get upset because I tell you the truth.

I didn't want anything only to see how your date went, but I see it didn't go as plan. So since I'm bothering you I'll let yo ass go!" "Bye," said Angie as she was hanging up the phone.

Angie hanging up so abruptly had Rachael thinking about what she said. *Umm I haven't spoken to DC since the date let me give her a call.* Rachael picked up the phone and dialed DC's number.

"You've reached DC"

Damn her voice thought Rachael as she hung up*, man I wonder if Angie is right?*

CHAPTER 6

Glad to be leaving work Ming couldn't wait to get home. She was exhausted and she missed her woman, she hadn't talked to Kimoni in a few days and she wanted to feel the warmth of her body. Just as she was thinking nasty thoughts, Kimoni called.

"Hey, my baby," Kimoni greeted Ming when she answered the phone

"Hello there, my sweetheart I was just thinking of you in such a naughty way," Ming confessed.

"Now were you Kimoni asked, tell me what's on your mind and all those nasty little dirty thoughts."

"Umm, how about I just come and show you, that would be so much better," teased Ming.

"Oh shit, yes it would be better for the both of us, so I will be eagerly waiting for you," declared Kimoni.

"Sounds like what I need, I'm on my way," announced Ming.

"Ok baby see you in a few," and the two hung up.

Ming arrived at Kimoni's in less than twenty minutes. "Hello, I'm here to see Ms. Grey," she told the doorman.

"Hello Ms. Foster, Ms. Grey is expecting you go head up."

"Thank you," Ming the proceeded to the elevator and got on she pushed the button for Kimoni's floor. *Oh I can't wait to take these shoes off,* she thought as the elevator door opened. Ming made her way to Kimoni's place and rang the doorbell.

"Well hello my sweet, get on in here," Kimoni directed.

"Yes daddy," beamed Ming as she walked in and planted a quick kiss on Kimoni's lips.

"Give me your briefcase baby," Kimoni told Ming. Doing as she was asked Ming gave Kimoni her briefcase. Kimoni then sat the briefcase in the corner and took Ming by the hand and lead her to the bedroom.

"How was work?" Kimoni asked Ming as she kissed her hand.

"It was wonderful baby and how was your day," Ming asked?

"Just business baby but now it's going to end great with pleasure," revealed Kimoni.

"Oh is it now," teased Ming.

"Umm hum, let me show you." Kimoni walked Ming into her master bathroom suite that was illuminated with candles. As Kimoni stared into Ming's eyes she began to unbutton Ming's shirt. Never once taking her eyes off Ming she then began to unzip her skirt. Now fully exposed in only her underwear Kimoni knells down to help Ming out of her shoes and stockings. Taking her hands and rubbing her legs from her ankle to her waist. Kimoni then picked Ming up and placed her on the counter top as she glides in between Ming's legs and the two starts to kiss passionately. Kimoni takes her hands and begins to unfasten Ming's bra. Her perfect brown nipples hard with excitement scream for attention as they bounce out her bra, Kimoni begins to caress Ming's nipples with her finger tips. Ming let out a purr and tossed her head back in delight.

"Oh baby yes, we missed you so!" Ming whispered.

Wanting to feel the wetness of her, Kimoni opened Ming's legs slightly to gain access to her pleasure treasure. Using her right hand Kimoni found Ming's wet spot and begins to rub her clit between her fingers very slowly and sensually. Each caress made Ming's anticipation grow. Kimoni gently inserts her finger and rubbed circles on the inside of her pussy while she kissed Ming with fiery. Taking their passion to the next level Kimoni inserts another finger and with her left hand she pulled Ming in close. With slow and steady thrust Kimoni's fingers conquered Ming's pussy!

"You like that baby," she whispered in Ming's ear?

"Yes" whimpered Ming.

"Y…..e…..s…."

Getting pleasure from giving Ming pleasure Kimoni felt her excitement level rise. She craved to have Ming's nipples in her mouth she began to squeeze tease and lick Ming's breast nourishing that craving. Ming's breasts were so beautiful and tasty, suckling and fingering Ming made Kimoni wetter and wetter. She wanted Ming to release so that she could taste her juice.

"I, I, I Ming cried softly, baby you making me cum."

That was music to Kimoni's ears, "are you baby, give it to me then," Kimoni commanded Ming!

"Oh, oh sss," Ming cried as Kimoni fingered her harder and sucked on her nipples.

"I'm cuming baby I'm cuming baby," Ming gasped she then gripped the back of Kimoni's neck as her body reached climax.

Kimoni gradually takes her hand out of Ming's pussy and puts her fingers in her mouth to taste all that is her baby. After licking every ounce of juice that was left on her fingers, Kimoni and Ming shared a passionate kiss. Kimoni picked Ming up off the counter and walked her to the tub it was already filled with bubbles and soaking hot water. Kimoni helped Ming in first.

"Relax baby I'll be right back," she told Ming.

Kimoni left out the bathroom and when she returned she had two glasses of wine. Handing Ming the glasses Kimoni took off her robe and joined Ming in the water.

"The water is just right," Kimoni said.

"Yes baby it is, just like you like it," added Ming as she handed Kimoni her glass.

"Let's toast," said Ming as she raised her glass, "To us and lucky we are to have found one another!"

"Hear, hear," said Kimoni the two then clicked their glasses they then shared a brief kiss before they drank their wine.

CHAPTER 7

The ringing of Stony's phone startled her, she hadn't realized how late it was because she was busy making PG's soup and trying out a new recipe.

It was Ray calling.

"Hey man what's up," Ray said, when Stony picked up the phone.

"Hey, I called your ass hours ago man, but anyway I went to the store today and saw PG she's not looking to good man."

"I know replied Ray, I've been thinking the same thing I think it's more than what she's letting on."

"Yeah, I agree said Stony it maybe be nothing at all or something to worry about, but neither the less she needs to take her ass to the doctor."

"I told her the same thing man said Ray, but you know how PG gets."

"Yes I do, I'm all too familiar with it, but hey I called you so you could meet me over at her house. When I went to her store today she asked me to fix her some soup, so I'll be taking it over in about an hour."

"Ok cool I'll meet you over there and then maybe we can talk her into going to the doctor," replied Ray.

"Yes! That's exactly my thought so I'll see you in a few. One hour to be precise," Stony advised Ray.

"Ok I'm there," replied Ray and the two friends hung up the phone.

Ray and Stony arrived at PG's place simultaneously.

"Perfect timing," Ray said to Stony as they walked up to PG's door.

"Yes, it is, I'm always right on time," Stony responded the two friends started to laugh and give each other dap.

"I'm going to use the extra key so PG won't have to get up and open the door," Ray informed Stony.

Ray called out to PG when she opened the door, "PG its Ray and Stony where you at?"

"I'm in the living room man, and why are you yelling I'm sick not deaf!"

"You still got that smart-ass mouth being sick didn't stop that," Stony said laughing as she walked pass the living room into the kitchen to put the soup on the stove.

"Wasn't no body yelling," said Ray as she walked into the living room where PG was sitting in her lounge chair. "I needed to make sure you heard us while we were coming in."

"I did and so did my neighbors," said PG

"Whatever man, seem like your ass ok with all the shit you talking. Hey Stony, don't fix this mofo no soup ain't nothing wrong with her ass," Ray yelled into the kitchen.

"Don't play with me, I'm getting some of that soup I told you I was ok. I just had a bug or something."

"Naw, you the bug," Stony said as she walked in the living room with the tray of soup.

Yo ass got jokes to G," asked PG?

"Yep sholl do," replied Stony.

"Just feed me, give me the soup!" commanded PG.

Laughing, Stony hands PG the tray.

"Where's mine, I don't get a tray?" quizzed Ray

"Hell naw man, you not sick you better go help yourself."

"See this is a shame what I gotta do to get some food around here?" Ray said as she walked to the kitchen.

"Get sick," Stony yelled as Ray walked out the room.

All three friends started to laugh!

"Man this soup is good," Ray shouted from the kitchen.

"Don't be eating out the pot Ray!" Both PG and Stony yelled.

"I'm not, damn y'all I got a bowl," Ray said as she walked back in the living room to show them. "So how is your belly," Ray asked?

"Yeah, Stony interjected how are you feeling?"

"I'm cool just a little tired but I'll be shaking this bug soon trust me," replied PG.

"I hope so cause if you don't we will be dragging yo ass to the hospital said Stony."

"Kicking and screaming don't matter," added Ray.

"I hear ya'll but I'm good trust me," said PG as she finished eating her soup. Here before I forget, PG went in her pocket and then handed Stony the money she spent in the store.

"What's this," she asked PG puzzled?

"We boyz and your money isn't good at the store, we hold each other down so thanks for the soup and here's your money back."

Surprised at the message on her cell phone Nayla still wasn't ready to try and meet up with her family. It had been weeks since she came out, and her sister wanted to meet up and talk. Perhaps understand, *understand what* thought Nayla as she listened to the voice mail again. There isn't anything to understand *"I Love Pussy"* period! Why even try, they are so closed minded, "I'm not going to waste my time with anyone who can't accept me! I've lived a lie long enough," shouted Nayla.

Nayla deleted the voice mail she then dialed Ming's number.

"Hello there my sweet," Ming greeted Nayla.

"What's up baby Nayla responded what'ch doing?"

"Packing, getting ready for a business trip out of town why," Ming asked?

"When do you leave and when are you coming back," Nayla asked?

"In a couple of days and I leave in a few hours, why quizzed Ming everything ok?"

"I was just asking, when you make it safe call and let me know you're ok," declared Nayla.

"I will, so how have you been are things ok with you, have you spoke to your family yet?"

"I'm fine and no I haven't spoken with them yet. I've been working, working, working. Keeping busy that's all so much on my mind but enough about my sad story. Tell me about you and that new girlfriend of yours," Nayla asked slyly?

"Oh girl things are so wonderful Kimoni has been a dream and more. But we are taking things slow," Ming cautioned.

"That I do understand, noted Nayla you don't want to crash and burn especially since dating a stud is all new to you."

"Exactly asserted Ming and I certainly wouldn't want to be let down by expecting to much."

"I hear you babe, I hear you well let me let you finish cause I have a whole bunch of nothing to do," Nayla said laughing.

"Girl you are nuts I love you and I'll call you once I land, go ahead and get back to your nothing," bye Ming teased.

After hanging up with Ming Nayla thought about her family situation. "Should I call my sister back, hell they didn't want to deal with it until it slapped them in the face."

Ming was so happy to be touching down, "oh how I hated to fly. Something about the roar of the engine sent chills through me, plus the fact this big ass metal machine all up in the air with nothing holding it up!" But she made it safe to the Twin Cities and that she was grateful for. Ming arrived a day early to prepare and settle in for her meeting with Ms. Banks while walking through the airport Ming texted Nayla.

"I'm here safe and sound call you later try and be good"!

After texting Nayla Ming called her love bug.

"Hi there baby you made it safe," Kimoni asked?

"Yes replied Ming I'm walking to get my luggage and maybe I'll hit the Mall of America after I check into the hotel."

"Sounds good baby, just keep me in the loop and if you need me just call."

"Ok I will, I'll talk to you later," said Ming.

"Ok baby bye," said Kimoni and the two hung up the phone.

After hanging up with Ming Kimoni called DC.

"Hey what's up man?" DC greeted.

"Nothing just calling to see what's going on with you and to see how your date went the other day," replied Kimoni.

"Man it was ok, naw it was a semi disaster!" DC then begin to describe what happen to Kimoni.

"You bull shitting," blurted Kimoni!

"Hell no answered DC, I wish I was I just don't know man."

"Maybe you're over reacting some people just don't know how to pray out loud. Don't just go off that," Kimoni asserted.

"I'm trying not to but with every waking moment it seems like she isn't what I need in my life. Don't get me wrong she's beautiful, smart, seems to have a lot of ambition but she's just so damn shallow. You're lucky you found Ming and on the side of the road no doubt!"

"Yea bro I know and I must say it's going good so far, we're taking it slow and man slow feels good. Who knows where this could go I finally may have found my match," Kimoni surmised.

"Exactly," exclaimed DC! That's what I mean finding someone to match you in every way. That's that shit I'm looking for I'm going to be patient and try again with Rachael and if it doesn't work out with her then ol well!"

"Sounds like the thing to do, why don't you call her up and you guys have a quite date somewhere," Kimoni suggested.

"Yeah man I may, I'm just not sure though, but I'll hit you later I'm about to go and work out," crowed DC.

"Cool man talk with you later," the two hung up.

DC went to the gym in her building she wanted to lift some weights to clear her mind about the whole Rachael situation. After working out and clearing her mind DC decided to try it again with Rachael. *Maybe I'm being to judgmental* DC rationalized. *I'll give her a call later and let's just see how it goes,* she reveried. DC started the shower and then got in.

CHAPTER 8

While fixing herself a bowl of ice cream DC ran across Rachael's mind it had been a few days since their date and she hadn't seen nor heard from DC. *Should I call her* she thought to herself *I don't want to seem like I'm a groupie.* "I am Rachael Wilson I don't chase women, women chase me," she said out loud! Just as Rachael was getting ready to put her phone on the charger it rang.

It was DC, Rachael picked up right away, "hello" she answered.

"Hi Rachael, how are you" DC asked?

"I'm good and how are you doing" Rachael asked?

"Blessed replied DC, I wanted to know if you would be free tomorrow afternoon."

"I should be, what time" Rachael inquired?

"2 o'clock how does that sound" DC asked?

"Good, now wear something very comfortable and if you have some flats wear them," DC told Rachael.

"Flats why?" Fretted Rachael.

"Well I want you to be comfortable and it's a surprise so you will see tomorrow ok" repeated DC.

"Ok well, I need to prepare myself for tomorrow so let me go so I can get things ready" Rachael expressed.

"You do that sweets and I'll be by your place tomorrow at 2, see you then" DC confirmed.

Rachael woke up excited about her date with DC, she decided to give her magic spot extra treatment with a little wax job. She wanted to be prepared just in case she had a visitor there tonight.

After waxing and shaving Rachael gave herself a facial, since she had to wait thirty minutes before she could wash it off she decided to call Angie.

"Yes, what can I do for you," Angie inquired?

"Hey I called you to tell your ass that DC and I are going on a date today at two. So I guess you were wrong and I was right."

"Well congratulations I'm happy for you, now is that all you called me for" quizzed Angie?

"Yes, it sure is" replied Rachael!

"Well get the hell off my phone call me when the date is done, maybe you'll get lucky and DC will fuck you" chuckled Angie.

"Whatever, bye" and Rachael hung up her phone. Not caring nothing about what the hell Angie was talking about Rachael continued with her beauty regiment she was going to look flawless for DC.

DC knew that she ran the risk of being recognized on her date with Rachael this afternoon. She was cool with that she wanted to see how Rachael would react to people wanting her attention. Most women can't deal with, or be in a relationship with someone who is famous and it can become a bit much for them to bear.

Peeking out her window Rachael saw DC pulled up after a few moments her cell phone rang.

"Hi DC," Rachael greeted.

"Hello there Ms. Lady I'm outside waiting on you beautiful."

"Ok I'll be right out just let me grab my purse."

******

While doing her routine cleaning a feeling of despair over came Nayla, she all of a sudden had a sinking feeling in her stomach. "*Umm,* she thought, *I wonder what it could be?* Trying to shake the uneasy feeling she was experiencing Nayla decide to take a drive "*maybe that would help to clear my mind,* she thought."

Nayla got in her car with no clear destination just the open road, looking down at her gas hand she decided to get gas before she ran out. After getting her gas and pulling out the station Nayla got a call from her sister. She hit ignore on her phone and twenty seconds later she received a text message.

"YOU NEED TO COME BY MOM'S HOUSE IT'S AN EMERGENCY"

Something must have happened to my mom, she thought to herself." Nayla raced to her mom's place. When she pulled up she barely put the car in park and turned off the engine before she hopped out. Nayla ran up the stairs and turned the knob on the door it was already open.

"Mom!" Nayla called out when she walked in.

"In here, we're in the den," her sister answered.

Nayla's heart raced as she thought what could have happened to her mom. *Maybe she's sick, who knows,* but whatever it was she was anxious to find out. Upon entering the den Nayla saw that her mother was fine. Seated amongst her was her sister and her aunt, they were all waiting for her to arrive.

"Hey there baby" her aunt Pat greeted her.

"Hi, Aunt Pat" Nayla repeated as she fully entered the room, "hello" she addressed her mom and sister.

"Come on sit right here," her aunt directed that she sit close to her.

"Well I know you're wondering why you're here," her sister opened up the conversation.

Nodding her head yes Nayla answered "of course."

"Well since you did that poem…"

"No, you mean came out" Nayla interrupted her sister.

"Ok, came out if that's what you call it" Nayla sister rolled her eyes.

"If you're going to disrespect me and my life Nayla interjected then I'm out of here!"

"No one is trying to disrespect you baby in any kind of way," Aunt Pat countered. "We just want to have a clear understanding."

"What is there to understand," protested Nayla? "I don't like men, I love women plain, simple and direct!"

"Oh Lord Jesus no! Please help take this sin from my child," pleaded Nayla's mom.

"Take this sin from me, take this sin from me!" Nayla blurted again, "my lively hood is not a sin." "I can't change who I love and whom I'm attracted to! You all have no idea what it is like to live in a world where everyone including your own family despises who you are. Not understanding the feelings within, those feelings that are comfortable to you but make everyone else uncomfortable. I'm sick of living my life to please everyone but me," yelled Nayla!

"Baby all we have to do is get the Reverend down here and we can pray this devil out of you. We did it before and it worked," coaxed Nayla's mother.

"It worked," taunted Nayla. "No, the hell it didn't! All it did was make my life a living hell. It made me live in fear, disgust, torment, anguish the list goes on and on. You have no fucking idea what your so called praying the devil out did to me!"

"Don't use that kind of language in my house!" Nayla's mother got up out her seat to approach her.

"Wait a minute things are getting out of control, let's calm down," aunt Pat pleaded with everyone.

"No, what is out of control is that you all don't understand nor do you care to understand I'm still the same person. Nothing has changed other than I'm happier and

I'm free because I chose to be me and not the person you all want and think I should be," emphasized Nayla.

Looking at her sister Nayla asked, "you know the feeling you get when you think about lesbians and gays. That feeling of disgust and yuck well that's the same feeling I get when I think about being with a man."

"But why her sister asked?"

"Why do you like men? Right you can't answer that can you, you just do. So guess what, ask GOD why he choose me to be the gay sheep of this family because I didn't chose this. Who in their right mind would want this for their life! No damn support, nothing but hate everywhere and being in a family like this only makes my life worst. I can't change who I am. So, until you decide when and if to accept me Nayla Lynn Ivy for whom GOD created me to be then I'll rather be with those who are not blood who accept me not matter what!"

Looking around the room at her family "don't call me until you all can fully accept me!" Nayla avowed. "Goodbye," Nayla walked out the den and out the door of her mom's house slamming the door hard enough that it didn't close. With tears streaming down her face she got in her car and drove away. So distraught and upset Nayla pulled into the first parking lot she saw and cried her eyes out.

DC was standing on the passenger side of her car when Rachael came out her house. "Afternoon gorgeous" DC greeted Rachael.

"Well hello there stunning" Rachael responded as she walked towards DC to get in the car.

"Let's ride" said DC as she closed the car door once Rachael got inside.

DC and Rachael arrived at their destination The Daishay Aquarium, *wow* Rachael thought, *it's been years since I've been here.* As they made their way to admissions there was a burst of life waiting to get in.

"Hi are you DC?" A group of young ladies asked.

"Yes I am" DC replied.

"Oh my God" they begin to scream "can we please have your autograph we love you please, please, please!"

"Sure no problem, just stop screaming" DC laughed.

"You are our favorite stud model," one of the girls said!

"Yes and we are so shocked to see you here like OMG," another one chimed in.

"Well it's my pleasure ladies, you all have a good day" DC said as she finished signing her autograph for the group of ladies.

"Can we please take a picture with you?" Another lady from the group asked.

"Sure," DC turned to Rachael and smiled. "Do you mind taking the picture she asked?"

"No, not at all" Rachael answered as she took the camera from the lady so she could take the picture. "Now smile everyone" she announced right before she hit the button.

"Thank you so much" the ladies said to both DC and Rachael as they took off.

"The life of a model, thank you for understanding" DC said to Rachael smiling.

"You're welcome thanks for bringing me here, why are you smiling" Rachael asked?

"Well to respond to your first statement you're welcome and for your second question. I'm smiling at your beauty I just want to enjoy this day with you."

"And we shall so let's go see JAWS" jested Rachael!

"Ha, ha, ha, you got jokes today, cool lead the way my lady" ordered DC.

The ladies made their way to the Jellyfish exhibit first. As they walked close to the tank DC was drawn in by the Jellyfish beauty.

"They are so mysterious DC turned and said to Rachael." "Simple yet complex and so many different species."

"Well they look like mushrooms with strings attached to them" Rachael commented.

"Those are the tentacles which can be venomous depending the species, and if it stings you can die" DC informed Rachael.

"Oh really well I'll make sure I stay far away from them" said Rachael.

"You and me both" laughed DC, "you and me both!"

The two ladies then made their way to the Caribbean Reef Exhibit. There they got to see a Green Moray Eel, Sting Rays, Parrot Fish, and a Giant Sea Turtle.

"So how are you enjoying yourself" DC asked Rachael?

"I'm having a good time, it's nice" Rachael answered.

"Well I'm glad you are! So let's go see the Giant Octopus" beamed DC.

"Giant octopus oh no interjected Rachael, the only time I want to see that is when I am eating his cousin calamari!"

Girl whatever" responded DC as she grabbed Rachael's hand and led the way to the next exhibit. DC and Rachael exchanged small talk as they watched the sea life behind the glass. "Well I have one more treat for you" DC told Rachael. "Let's go to the concession stand and get some snacks and then we'll be off to see what I have in store."

I wonder what kind of treat it is, because I'm ready to get out of here, Rachael thought to herself.

While walking to the concession stand the ladies ran into True.

"Well hello," DC greeted True enthusiastically.

"Hey there you," True said as she moved in to give DC a hug. "What are you doing her she asked?"

"I was going to ask you the same thing, I'm here with Rachael" DC revealed as she turned to introduce the two. "Rachael this is Tameko my hair dresser, Tameko this is my friend Rachael."

"Hello Tameko" Rachael smirked as she extended her hand.

"Hi, Rachael, it's so nice to meet you" replied True as she shook Rachael's hand.

Just as the ladies were about to converse two kids ran up excitedly to True and said "come on come on the show is getting ready to start."

"Ok you guys, but that was rude of you what are you supposed to say when a person is talking and you want to gain their attention?"

"We're sorry we are supposed to say excuse me" the two kids chimed in unison.

"This is what I'm doing here" snickered True to DC and Rachael as she grabbed the two kids hands and held them up.

"I didn't know you had kids?" Surmised DC.

"Oh no I don't these are my nieces. I'm taking them to see the dolphin show and the other exhibits."

"Oh cool, maybe we can all sit together that's where Rachael and I are on our way to."

With a look of surprise on her face "that's the treat, the dolphin show" Rachael inquired?

"Yes," replied "DC is that a problem?"

"No, no not at all" stuttered Rachael.

"Oh ok, because you don't look like it's ok"

"I'm just surprised that's all I thought we were leaving it's fine and it's not a problem" declared Rachael trying to defuse the situation.

Turning back to True "I'll see you later" replied DC.

"Yeah just call me or something, nice to meet you" True addressed Rachael as she and her nieces walked off.

"So what would you like from the concession stand" DC asked Rachael?

"I'll have a blue slurpy and some popcorn please" answered Rachael.

"Ok I'll be right back"

As DC walked away "damn" Rachael thought! *I don't want to spend what little time I have with DC with some brats and their hairdresser ass aunt.*

"Hey you ready?" DC calling out to Rachael snapped her out of her daydream.

"Sure am which way are we going" Rachael asked?

"This way my dear" DC answered as she pointed to the entrance of the show.

When DC and Rachael enter the aquarium, there was a crowd of people sitting waiting for the show to begin. Trying to scan around to see two seats together DC spotted True. *Damn! True was looking good,"* she ruminated to herself and seeing her interact with her nieces made DC smile.

"Over there are two seats" Rachael pointed out in the opposite direction of where DC was looking.

"Since you spotted them lead the way" DC instructed Rachael.

Rachael was so glad to be on the opposite side of the show she didn't want True and DC anywhere near each other! She wanted all her time with DC to be alone and uninterrupted.

The ladies reached their seats and got ready to enjoy the show.

Once the show was over the ladies made their way out of the aquarium. While walking to DC's car they engaged in small talk. DC was really trying to find something that peaked Rachael interest besides spending money.

"I hope you enjoyed yourself today, did you?" DC asked Rachael as they pulled up in front of her place.

"Yes, I did, it was nice, very different I never expected to go see fish for a date" Rachael told DC.

"Well that's me always different, you never know what I'll have up my sleeve. I enjoyed your company and I hope you enjoyed mine." "You did enjoy mine" DC inquired playfully?

"Yes, I enjoyed your company always, and thanks for taking me. I better get in the house and let you get going, unless you would like to come in" asked Rachael?

"Thanks for the offer but I need to get home myself, but let me get that door for you." DC got out the car and ran to the passenger side to open the door. As Rachael got out she thanked DC one more time for the date as she made her way to her door.

DC went back and got in her car and to watch Rachael as she went safely inside. Before she closed her door Rachael waved goodbye to DC before she drove off.

Once inside Rachael called Angie to come over. She needed to speak to her about her date with DC and much as she hated to admit it she needed to get some advice from her!

"Hey Angie, its Rachael I need you to come by right now!"

CHAPTER 9

Sitting in the doctor's office seemed like an eternity. PG hated the doctor with a passion the gyno especially! Those little ass robes they made you wear, and all the touching and probing was against her religion.

"Hello there Ms. Glover" the doctor greeted PG as she entered the exam room. "Long time no see, where have you been and what have you been up to?"

"Hey doc, I've been fine, just trying to take care of myself as directed." "How are you doing" PG asked?

"I'm good thanks" replied the doctor, "so tell me what brings you in today she asked?"

"For the last couple of days I haven't been feeling well."

"Really," responded the doctor as she begins to take notes.

"Yes" sighed PG as she began to explain her symptoms and what had been going on with her for the last few days.

The doctor continued to took notes as she listens attentively to everything that PG had to say. Once PG was done talking the doctor began to do a thorough exam. She checked PG from head to toe.

"Ok" the doctor said once she was done with the physical exam. "I'm going to have my nurse come in and draw some blood from you, so that we can send it to the lab I want to check all possibilities. Right now it looks like you are dehydrated and exhausted. It just may be a case of influenza but I want to make for certain. After the nurse is finish drawing your blood I want you to go over to the radiology department and have an ultra sound and maybe even a CT scan completed. I want to check to see if you have gallstones"

"Gallstones, PG repeated, you think it's just that she asked?"

"I would rather be safe than sorry, you have had your symptoms for quite some time and I want to make sure nothing else has developed," the doctor explained to PG. "It's just a precaution to make sure I don't miss anything. You know with your illness we have to take ever thing serious and with that being said if you do have them we are going to have to do surgery to remove them."

"Damn, surgery is the last thing I want doc" exclaimed PG!

"I know you don't, but let's not focus on that right now. What I need you to do is start eating right if you haven't been. I need you to start on a low-fat diet to reduce any risk of developing anything just in case you do have them."

"Ok, Ok, but what are the risk involved for the surgery" PG inquired?

"As with any surgery there are risks involved but you know we must make special precautions for you. But as I said let's not get ahead of ourselves let's see what comes back from your test and we take it from there ok." The doctor then finished writing up the notice for the lab work. "The results will be in within 24 hours after you take them and either way I will give you a call. If in fact you just developed the flu will deal with that. But I am going to need for you get some rest and don't over exert yourself. Ok Ms. Glover?"

"Yes," answered PG.

"Ok then try not to think about it or worry, I need for you to drink plenty of fluids. You need to replenish nutrients that you lost so that you can get your strength up so please Ms. Glover, once again no work just rest! I'm going to write you up a prescription for some pain medications and some antibiotic as a precaution and have it sent to the pharmacy. I'll be talking to you soon." The doctor then left out of the exam room.

PG sat on the doctors table not knowing what to think. The doctor really had put so much on her mind. She had been doing so well to prevent herself from having an episode. The nurse knocking on the door to come in took PG out of her thoughts. "Come in" PG commanded.

"Hi Ms. Glover," the nurse greeted. "I'm Sheri and I will be drawing your blood."

"Hi Sheri, nice to meet you responded PG, which arm do you need?"

"It doesn't matter either one will do just fine" as the nurse prepped PG the two continued to make small talk. The nurse could sense PG nervousness and she wanted to put her mind at ease.

"Ok all done," announced the nurse as she filled the last vile with blood.

"Wow that was quick and painless." declared PG.

"I try to be," replied the nurse I don't want the patient in any unnecessary pain.

"Thank you for making me comfortable because when you're stuck as many time as I've been you just brace for the pain," revealed PG.

"I know replied the nurse I could tell, so I need for you to get dress and go to the 3rd floor and have your other test completed. Once they are done with your test you are finished for the day and when the results come back the doctor will give you a call. Do you have any questions the nurse asked?"

"No and thank you for all your help, guess I'll see you next time" PG answered.

As the nurse left the room and closed the door PG thought about should she go straight home or to work just for a few hours, she was tired and wanted to sleep like the doctor had order. But she needed to lay eyes on her baby "Frames" off to work I go, once I completed all of the test I need to have done she decided, against the doctor's orders.

When PG made it to the store it was very busy. A sight she always loved to see, PG eased in without being noticed so she thought. She didn't feel like chatting she just wanted to check up on things and go home. While walking to her office PG was greeted by Ray.

"Hey man wha'cha doing here" PG asked?

"Checking up on you didn't you have a doctor's appointment," inquired Ray?

"Yeah I did" PG replied.

"Ok," chided Ray!

"Ok what" grumbled PG?

"Don't play with me," Ray warned PG. "What happened, what did she say?"

"Well she took some blood and had me go do a CT scan and an ultra sound to make sure I don't have gallstones."

"Really, so when will the results be back," Ray quizzed?

I'm not really sure when the results will come back but the doctor said they should be in shortly either way she is going to give me a call" explained PG.

"Ok well when and if you have to go back to the doctor I'm going with you, and I don't want to hear any bullshit" Ray declared!

"Ok, ok," conceded PG. "You won't get no bullshit and I'll let you know."

"You better or there will be hell to pay," threaten Ray. "I think you need to call Tony."

"No, not yet not until after I get the results there is no need to worry anyone else yet."

"Well if you won't call Tony, at least let Stony know then. Someone else besides me needs to know what's going on."

"You right, but Stoney that's it, until the results come in." PG then dialed Stoney number to let her know what happened at the doctor.

******

Ming was happy to be on her way home. Looking at her watch, *great that hour delay put a monkey wrench in my plans*, she thought. She wanted to be home by at least 5pm no later than 6pm. But now it looks like she wouldn't make it until after 7. *I guess I'll have to wait until tomorrow to make any calls,* she said to herself while exiting the plane Ming saw a couple with a baby. *Oh, I want a baby* the thought ran across her mind, but just as quick as it came it left faster!

Making her way to baggage claim Ming took in the wonderful feeling that she had closed yet another big deal. Since taking DC as a client Ming had worked her magic to get her the best deals and nothing less. After retrieving her luggage, she headed to the front of the airport. Kimoni had arranged for a car to pick her up and take her home.

"Ms. Foster?" the driver quizzes as Ming approached the car.

"That would be I," Ming replied.

The driver opened the door and helped Ming inside. Once in the car the driver took Ming's luggage and put it in the trunk.

On the ride home Ming called Kimoni to let her know that she made it back to Chicago and was on her way home.

"Hey you" Ming greeted Kimoni when she picked up the phone.

"Hello baby I've been waiting for your call. Are you on your way home" Kimoni asked?

"Yes love I'm in the car" now Ming replied.

"Good baby, would you like some company tonight" Kimoni inquired?

"Why yes of course, I would love some" Ming beamed!

"Ok baby I will be there within the hour are you hungry?"

"Slightly if you get something make it light nothing to heavy" advised Ming.

"Ok baby light so I'll see you momentarily."

After they hung Ming wanted to check on Nayla so she gave her a call. Nayla didn't answer so Ming sent her a text

"Thinking of you love, I'm back in town in route home. Call me tomorrow love Ming."

After sending the text Ming sat back and relaxed for the rest of the ride home. She couldn't wait to see her woman, and take a long hot bath and with some luck Kimoni would join her.

It had been a few days since the confrontation Nayla had with her family. *Damn these muthafuckers will drive you to drink! Thank God for strength,* she thought. She saw the text from Ming but she wasn't able to respond she was running late and needed to head out.

Nayla gathered her belongings and out the door she went. Work was getting more demanding since she was being considered for a promotion and she wasn't going to let anything get in the way of that. She hadn't discussed what happen between her and her family with anyone. She just wanted to leave it behind her. She begins to whisper to herself, "they will never accept me and I just have to accept that! I just have to move on with my live and don't look back, it's their lost not mine. "I will continue to live my life as I see fit not as others see fit for me. I will be happy even if no one in my blood family is ever happy for me. I have a great group of close friends who are my family and have treated me better than my own family has at times. Why stress over those that choose not to be in your life because of their ignorance." One thing I have learned from being in the closet for so damn long is that you can never be free living for others! You have to be true to yourself and live life to the fullest because you are only blessed with one and once it's gone nothing can be made up. There is no going back to try to finish or relive the life God gave me, it's mine and I'm going to live how the hell I want!"

After a wonderful night of romantic bliss Ming arrived at work glowing!

"Well hello there La La La Ming. You looked like you got fucked real good last night" Angie teased.

With a look of satisfaction on her face Ming declared, "I so did! But that's none of your business right now you'll have to wait to hear about it at brunch laughed Ming!"

"It better be juicy since you making me wait so long" Angie warned.

With a sly look on her face "it sure is, it certainly is." "Now back to work lady, I need for you to get DC on the phone for me," she instructed Angie.

"Ok, right away boss." Doing as she was instructed Angie called DC.

Just as Ming walked into her office her phone was ringing. "Hello" she answered. "I have DC on line one Angie told her."

"Ok, thanks Ang put her through."

"Good morning DC," Ming greeted. "How are you on this fine morning," she asked?

"I'm great how about you," DC quizzed?

"I'm wonderful and I have some wonderful news for you as well," revealed Ming.

"Really, what is it" inquired DC?

"You have been chosen as the new face of Studware. It is a new clothing line by fashion designer Samantha Banks. She is a new and upcoming designer with a great eye for dressing the masculine women in our community. She will be debuting this line of clothing, so pack your bags you're going to New York for fashion week" revealed Ming!

"That's wonderful Ming thank you so much" exclaim DC! "When do I leave?"

"I'm going to contact Kimoni to make the final arrangements and she will contact you by the end the week to let you know."

"Sounds good answered DC, Ming I just want to tell you that I really appreciate all your hard work and everything you have done thus far for me!"

"No problem, that's what I do, I'm supposed to keep you happy. Now let me finish ironing out the details so you can be on your way. If I need you for anything I'll give you a call" concluded Ming.

"Ok talk to you later, bye" and DC hung up the phone.

DC was thrilled about going to New York she could now kill two birds with one stone. Business and pleasure have a little fun while taking care of business.

The wheels in DC mind began to spin.

The work week flew by and it was almost time for Sunday brunch. The ladies were meeting at Angie's house and it seemed like forever since the last time they were together for brunch.

"Umm... Angie this is good," Nayla commented

"Girl thanks but I didn't cook this I had it catered for you guys today."

"Oh that was nice, thank you" chimed Ming.

"You're welcome, I wanted us to come here for brunch so that we could really talk and be in a comfortable environment. I just wasn't in the mood to be in a restaurant," replied Angie.

"Me either" coaxed Nayla!

"So, you guys, I have an idea. I want to go on a mini vacation just to get away for a few days. So why don't we go to New York City," exclaimed Angie!

"Yes! I'm down I need to get the hell out of this city anyway." Nayla responded.

"Sure, that would be great when are you talking," Ming asked?

"ASAP! The sooner the better" Angie said.

"I don't know," Rachael added reluctantly. "Going away for a few days isn't a good idea for me right now. I'm trying to spend time with DC while she's here."

"And how has that been going?" Angie asked in a sarcastic tone.

"Girl please who cares about you and DC spending time. We're talking about getting away for a few days to have some fun in another city. Hell DC leaves the country you don't see her cry about leaving yo ass," chimed Nayla.

"Whatever," grumbled Rachael to Nayla. "When are you trying to go again" Rachael turned and asked Angie?

"In a few weeks let me check out some flights and hotels and I'll let you know" said Angie.

"New York, New York" cheered Nayla. "Here we come! I know a couple of lesbian spots we can hit."

Everyone turned and looked at Nayla in disbelief!

"WHAT! Shouted Ming. "How the hell do you know about lesbian spots in New York fresh out the closet?"

"Umm I just do, Nayla admitted laughing don't worry about all that. But when we do go it's this one spot we have to hit up."

"See that's that closet freak shit! I told y'all she was into some weird shit" Angie blurred while pointing at Nayla.

All the ladies laughed expect Rachael she wasn't sure if she wanted to go or not, she just wanted to spend all the free time she had with DC.

"Forget all of you I bet we have a good time," Nayla said smirking. "Just watch!"

"Well as soon as I find us a good deal I'll let you, now I have a question does anyone have a problem sharing a room?" "I need to know before I start looking" Angie asked?

"I need my own room Nayla raised her hand slowly, just in case I get lucky. I plan on having a wonderful time no holds barred!"

"Girl now you wanna live wild," Ming chuckled. "Go right ahead I just want to shop and party but nothing like what's on your nasty mind."

"Well I ain't mad at cha" declared Angie as she high fived Nayla. "Making up for all that closeted time umm" winked Angie.

"Well I need to share a suite with one of y'all" Angie confessed "Ming, Rachael which one of you got me?"

"I don't know if I'm going to go yet" Rachael let out a big sigh.

"What's wrong with you" asked Ming? "You've been in a funky mood since we been here spill it!"

"She's all upset about DC and how their dates haven't been going the way she wants them" Angie answered.

"Shut up Angie! Our dates have been fine I just would rather spend my free time with DC than in New York that's all" Rachael contended.

"Yeah, yeah" replied Angie.

"So you saying, you of all people don't want to go to New York to shop and hang out? Well suite yourself ok ladies I guess it's just us three" boasted Ming.

"Ok then Angie, I'll reserve Ms. Nasty Nayla her own room and you and I will be bunking together."

"Come on Rachael, come you'll have a blast! Trust it will get your mind off of DC," Nayla pleaded.

"Maybe, I'll let you know by mid-week."

"Great knuckle head, glad you're thinking about it" teased Angie. "Now let's watch a movie!"

"Yeah" Ming agreed as she got up to look through Angie's movie collection.

"What movie y'all wanna watch" Ming asked?

"Something with some" action Angie yelled.

"No, something with some hot sex scenes" emphasized Nayla.

"You, horny little toad" joked Ming. "What do you want to see" she asked Rachael?

"It doesn't matter I'll watch whatever" said Rachael.

121

"Man, this DC dilemma really has you acting differently" stated Nayla. "You've never acted this way over a woman before. What is really going on?"

"Yeah" Angie agreed. "What's going on truthfully?"

"Would you like to talk about it" asked Ming?

"No not really, I just don't understand" murmured Rachael!

"Understand what, that your ass is shallow" taunted Angie! "Now you've finally met someone who doesn't care about all that vain shit. You might as well chopped that up and move on cause you and DC nope it ain't gonna happen."

"Shut up Angie," Ming warned!

"Well it's the truth!" "I only state facts," Angie emphasized.

"Facts or not sometimes you need not to say everything that's on your mind" Nayla added.

"No it's cool y'all she right I may as well just chalk this one up" Rachael confessed as she took a sip of her drink.

"No matter we're here and we will always be here" Ming assured Rachael. The ladies then got up and gave Rachael a hug.

"Thanks guys, that's why I love y'all" declared Rachael.

"And we love you too" they all said in unison.

"Girl where did you get this food from" asked Nayla?

"Taste of the rainbow catering" Angie boasted with a grin.

"No you didn't" hollered Rachael!

"Are you stalking that chef now" jeered Ming?

"No, no, and no" Angie answered. "It just happened by chance. When I asked you guys over I didn't feel like cooking so I just placed an order."

"You sure you didn't try, to just get her over here to your place" laughed Rachael?

"Nope, and you would be proud of me Ming" Angie asserted. "I took your advice and I haven't been aggressive and it seems to be working. I've ran into Stony a few times."

"Wait, who is Stony?" Nayla interrupted looking confused.

"Stony is the caterer crazy" laughed Angie.

"Oh, ok carry on" responded Nayla.

"Yes, continue please" Ming chimed.

"I've just been toning it down and not being so forward, and even though it's quite hard, I'm enjoying the break from the hardcore in your face Angie. While getting to know this soft-spoken Angie."

"Where the hell is she" Rachael joked while looking around the room?

"Shut up! I thought you were still blue over DC" Angie teased. "But anyway, before I was rudely interrupted I just called into the store and placed the order that was it."

"All, look at you, I'm so proud" said Ming

"Why thank you, I'm trying" replied Angie

"Girl I don't know what for" joked Nayla. "You've been hardcore all this time, well I hope the old Angie comes back cause it's time to get wild and free baby, cause we're going to New York!"

CHAPTER 10

After finalizing all the plans with Kimoni DC decided to take Rachael to New York with her for fashion week. *Rachael is a high maintenance, high fashion kinda woman* DC thought. *She would really enjoy being there for the weekend to enjoy all of the designers and parties.*

"I'll make it romantic and intimate for us, maybe that will get her to open up and relax and not be so focused on non-meaningful things. Let me call her now and see if she can make it."

Rachael was feeling conflicted about if she should go to New York with her girls or if she should just keep trying with DC. To turn up the heat on their relationship/situation whatever you want to call it. *I have never had to work this hard for an RL,* she thought to herself. "I just don't get what's taking DC so long to open up and spend some money on me? I guess I'm going to have to regroup and come up with another strategy or break my number one rule! But whatever the case I need to get this thing to another level quick fast and in a hurry" she blurted out loud!

Just as Rachael was about to start brain storming her new plan for DC her phone rang.

"Hey there, I was just thinking about you" Rachael answered.

"Really? Were they happy, bad, naughty or nasty thoughts" DC teased.

"Umm let's just say they were some bad, naughty, little nasty thoughts that made me happy" Rachael revealed.

DC laughed, "ok then maybe one day you will divulge and let me in on those thoughts. But in the mean time I called to see how you were doing and to ask you a question."

"I'm good, can't complain," Rachael responded in the sincerest voice she could muster. Because deep inside she was a pure wreck but she couldn't let DC know that. "Sure, you can ask me anything, what's up" Rachael quizzed?

"Well I wanted to know if you would like to accompany me to NYC for a weekend getaway in a few weeks" inquired DC?

In a state of disbelief and shock Rachael paused for a moment and looked at her phone. "Umm what did you just ask me, have you been talking to Ming?"

"No, what are you talking about," DC asked dumb founded?

"You just brought up New York, and I was just talking to Ming, you know what never mind! The answer is yes, I would love to accompany you to New York for the weekend just tell me when and I'm there!"

"Great I'm glad you agreed to come, just to let you know we won't be flying out together. I'll be leaving before you but I will be at the airport to pick you up when you land" DC assured Rachael.

"Oh, by myself" Rachael sulked. "I would rather for you to be there with me."

"I know but unfortunately I can't, but trust me it will be worth that plane ride."

"Ok so what weekend are you speaking of" Rachael asked eagerly?

"In a few weeks, I'll let you know soon, so that you can make proper arrangements and such. Also, don't worry I will be paying all your expenses it's the least I can do since you will be traveling alone" said DC.

"Why thank you" Rachael tried to sound surprise, even though she was thinking you better had paid for my expenses! "That is so generous of you." But had DC not offered she was surly getting ready to ask.

"You're quite welcome just get ready to have a marvelous time, NYC is going to be great. Well I need to make a few other calls and arrangements," declared DC. "I will be in touch with you soon to give you all the flight info."

"Ok and thank you so much for inviting me, I can't wait until I hear from you again. Talk to you later and have a good night," Rachael said before she hung up the phone.

"Hell yes!" She screamed "New York City with DC what are the odds who would have ever thought! I wonder if Ming had something to do with this?" Rachael picked up the phone and dialed Ming's number.

Ming was on her way to pick up Nayla, as she was pulling up she saw the call from Rachael come in. Not wanting to be questioned about DC Ming sent the call to voicemail.

"Hey there" Nayla greeted Ming as she opened the car door to get in.

"What's happening" Ming responded back.

"Nothing much ready to get this shopping done so when we hit the NYC I'll be looking good, good," Nayla exclaimed.

"Girl you are a mess Ming laughed, hey Rachael just called me and I sent the call to voice mail. I don't want to hear any questions about DC you know what I mean."

"Yeah, I understand," Nayla agreed. "Rachael is just so used to getting what she wants."

"Exactly! And now that it's not going her way and DC is my client it makes for a very awkward situation with me in the middle. I don't want our friendship to suffer because she expects me to report DC's every move to her."

"Yeah and you know that's what she's going to expect, but you are going to have to let her know! But enough about her ass let's talk about how my ass is going to party, party, party when we get to New York," screamed Nayla!

"So how many stores will we be hitting" Ming asked Nayla?

"I don't know girl we are just going to shop till we drop" Nayla squeaked!

Ming just laughed to herself at how Nayla was getting her joy back since everything that happen. She was glad that Nayla was coming around to her old self but hell this was her new self because Ming had never seen her so free and just ready for the world!

Since Ming didn't pick up the phone Rachael decided to call Angie. Angie didn't answer the phone either, *damn I wonder where everyone is and what the hell are they doing without me*, Rachael thought to herself.

Just as she was about to put her phone day it rang back.

"Hey you just called?" Angie asked all out of breath.

"Yeah, I did, what are you doing that you are so out of breath?" "Please don't tell me you're screwing!" Rachael screamed.

"Nope, I wouldn't be able to speak words you could understand" Angie retorted.

"Whatever" Rachael chimed.

"Don't whatever me" Angie snapped! "You called me so what do you want! Spill it…"

"I just wanted to let you know that I will be going to New York, but not with you guys. DC has invited me to come and see her during fashion week" Rachael screamed all excited like a teenager.

"Whoopty damn do good for you! Now that you've announced that bye Rachael" and Angie hung up the phone.

Realizing that Angie had just hung up on her she just shook her head and said, "your ass is just jealous forget you!" "Let me get my suitcase and things together cause I'm going to see DC for fashion week in New York City!!!"

The weeks leading up to the NY trip flew by, everyone was excited about going.

Nayla wanted to get wild and have a good time, no questions asked. Ming wanted to kick back and have a good time with her girls, while Angie wanted and needed a change in scenery to get her mind clear and focused. Rachael of course was looking forward to the lights camera and action that was to come with being on DC's side!

DC hoped that taking Rachael to New York was a good idea. She had tried to get Rachael to see that the simple things in life were just as important as the finer things, if not more important. Because at any given time the finer things could be taken away.

DC had found out from Kimoni that Ming would be in New York with some friends at the same of the fashion show. DC wanted to surprise Rachael so she invited Ming and her friends to come to the show.

DC texted Ming to let her know how she wanted to surprise Rachael with her and her friends attending the fashion show. Ming told her what hotel she was staying in, DC then sent the tickets by messenger.

Ming was delighted to have received DC's text. She replied back promptly and she was so relieved to not have been in the middle of their developing relationship or non-relationship.

Cool, DC texted back as she walked into the airport to locate the gate to pick up Rachael. She took a deep breath for she knew it would be no turning back, and once she was seen publicly with her the flood gates would fly open. Social media, the press, everyone is going to want to know who is this woman?

Rachael was a little nervous as she exited the plane. She didn't know why she felt so anxious "hell I've flown all over the world why do I have so many butterflies," she said to herself. Just as she was about to take out her phone and call DC a voice called her name and then leaned in to kiss her.

"Hey beautiful how was your flight?"

"Wonderful but I'm happy to be off it, look at you" she told DC.

"Well I'm glad you made it safe sorry you couldn't come a little earlier in the week."

"I know but the call of duty wouldn't let me get away, but I made it in time for your event."

"Yes you did so are you ready for us to get the day started" DC asked?

"Yes I am, let's get my bags they are on the lower level," Rachael replied.

The two ladies walked to retrieve Rachael's luggage. "Are you hungry" DC quizzed?

"Famished, you have anything special in mind?"

"Whatever you want, your wish is my command" DC declared. "Let's get you checked into your hotel room and your bags put up. I have a couple of hours for us to hang out and then it's off to rehearsal."

"Ok, I can't wait to see you walk the runway" Rachael said excitedly.

"I'm glad that you could attend and I'm happy for you to see me work. I will have a big surprise for you the day of the fashion show and I hope it makes your day."

Umm I wonder if it's diamonds or something, I bet it's something real expensive. Rachael thinks to herself .

"You do?" Rachael said trying to act unbothered. "I can't wait to find out what it is, I know I will just love it!"

After retrieving Rachael's luggage, the ladies left the airport and made their way to the hotel so that Rachael could get checked in. Just as she promised DC paid the tab, the room was a beautiful Jr. Suite with the works.

"My goodness this room is beautiful, thank you DC" exclaim Rachael!

"No need to thank me you're quite welcome. Do you want to freshen up before we go get something to eat DC asked?"

"Yes, just give me a minute and I'll be ready."

"Ok do your thang I'll be out here waiting."

After a few minutes Rachael emerged from the bathroom looking radiate.

"Damn beautiful you make it look so easy with your fine ass" DC flirted. Will are you ready to go?"

"Why thank you but it is rather easy for me Rachael smiled, and yes I'm ready."

DC walked to the door and held it open for Rachael to go through. After making sure the door was securely locked the two ladies then walked to the elevator. Once down stairs they jumped in DC's car and headed to the restaurant.

Ming, Nayla, and Angie had been in NYC enjoying the sights, shows, along with shopping, shopping, and more shopping!

Ming was thrilled when DC texted her, she wanted to go to the fashion show. DC inviting her and the girls was a great idea. Just as she advised, the messenger arrived on time Ming went down to the front desk to pick up the package.

"Where have you been Missy?" Nayla asked as Ming walked back in the hotel suite.

"DC sent us tickets to her show we are going to surprise Rachael! So, if y'all talk to her today don't mention it agreed?"

"Agreed," both Nayla and Angie said in unison

"Well I hope it's not tonight because I have a great night planned already"!

"You do" asked Angie?

"Do tell quizzed Ming what do you have planned?"

"Well we can't come to the NYC and not see the "King" perform and tonight she has a show."

"The "King" squealed Angie excited! You mean, please tell me you mean, The King of Brooklyn wait to you see my…"

"Yes! Nayla interrupted, I'm talking the one and only. Ladies we have VIP seats for the show and I'm sure it's going to get dirty!" Nayla said with a sly look in her eye.

"Ooh, I can't wait" said Angie

"So do you have a ticket for Rachael?" asked Ming.

"No, I only got three, I'm quite sure she is going to be preoccupied with DC to even want to hang out with us!"

"Right agreed Angie plus we don't need her stuffy ass there spoiling our time with the King." She and Nayla being to dance around the room

"Well let's go and get us some food and whatever else, so we can get back here and get some rest for tonight" advised Ming.

CHAPTER 11

"The food was great exclaimed Rachael, I couldn't eat another bite."

"Not even a little dessert" DC teased.

"Umm it depends on who is on the menu oops, I mean what is on the menu."

The two ladies both begin to chuckle.

"Well since you can't eat another bite let's get out of here and see some of the sights." DC motioned for the waiter so she could pay the bill.

The ladies gathered their things and left the restaurant to start their day on the town.

After taking in the sights of NYC with Rachael it was almost time for DC to head to rehearsal for the show. "Hey, she said turning to Rachael as with all things time flies when you are having fun. Would you like to go back to your hotel room, go hang out with your friends that's here, or come with and watch me rehearse?"

"Well, would it be ok for me to come with you and watch you work your magic?"

"Sure I wouldn't have offered if it wasn't ok, I hope you are up for a long night these things can be brutal" DC warned.

"Doesn't matter, I don't mind, just being here in NYC and seeing the behind the scenes of your show is great. Do you think I'll be able to meet the designer or some other famous designers" Rachael asked?

Rachael question didn't sit well with DC. "Being worried about meeting a famous designer isn't why I brought you here" DC thought to herself. "There is no need to meet the designer when you're here with the famous model DC" said with a condescending tone.

Sensing a hint of annoyance Rachael tried to clean up her question. "Well of course you are all that matters and the reason for me being here. Whew don't blow it Rachael says to herself in her mind."

Not wanting to carry any type of negative energy to the rehearsal. DC chose to just let it go and focus on work.

When Nayla, Ming, and Angie stepped out the cab in front of club they all grew excited to be taking in the vibrant New York City life. "The Pool", Ming said looking up at the name of the club. "Yes" shrieked Nayla where the motto is "you are guaranteed to get wet, come on in". "My kind of club" Angie professed! "Let's do as instructed," Nayla said as the ladies made their way to the front entrance of the club. Because Nayla had paid for VIP they didn't have to wait in line, the three ladies were ushered in and directed up the stairs to the VIP area.

"Oh, this is nice" Angie said as she took a seat on the plush couch. Just as Nayla and Ming were about to sit down and agree, a woman with glistening chocolate skin and a perfect set of breasts with plumb ass to match. "Welcome to VIP, my name is Me'Lisa and I am one of your pleasure girls for the night. Please let me know if I can do anything for you. Would either one of you ladies like something to drink or eat?"

The ladies decided what they were going to eat and drink and they gave Me'Lisa their orders.

"Ok you guys I'll be right back with your drinks," Me'Lisa advised.

"Damn this club is the shit" Angie said as she jumped up from the couch and started shaking her ass to music.

"Yes, it is" said Nayla as she joined Angie dancing, the two friends begin to dance seductively and provocatively with each other. "Come on Ming join us" shouted Nayla. "Yeah boss lady make it a threesome or at least as close as your ass will get to one" laughed Angie!

"No thank Ming declined I'm fine watching the show of you two, y'all don't need my help."

Just a Ming was saying no Nayla backed up and begin to gyrate her ass in Ming's direction. "You know you want it" Nayla teased as she lifted her skirt playfully showing her bare ass to Ming.

"Girl where the hell are your drawers?" Ming asked shocked!

"Don't worry about that my friend I've prepared, I plan on getting lucky tonight. I'm in New York, single, free, and a non-closeted lesbian. It's time!"

"Girl you a damn mess" exclaim Ming!

"Good our drinks are coming" Angie said out of breath as she walked up to both Ming and Nayla.

Me'Lisa the pleasure girl was walking up with the ladies' drink order. "Here you are ladies your drinks are ready." Me'Lisa then begin to pass around their unique order. "Ok is there anything else you ladies need?" she asked.

"Yes, can you please bring me a glass or a bottle of water?" Angie instructed.

"I sure can, I'll be right back," Me'Lisa then left to go and retrieve the water for Angie.

"Let's toast beamed Nayla to true and genuine friendships, to living free and being happy! I want you guys to know how much I appreciate you both, you are more than my friends you are my sister's and I love you both dearly! Now let's party."

"Here, here" said Ming

"I'll drink to that!" said Angie

The ladies clinked their glasses together and took a sip of their drinks

"Oh that's my song" yelled Nayla as she took sip of her drink and then sat it down. "Watch my drink boo, I'll be right back" she instructed Ming. "Come on" Angie she said as she took her by the hand and led her to the dance floor.

Ming just shook her head and laughed at her friends, "Don't hurt nobody" she shouted after them.

"We will" Nayla replied as they disappeared down the stairs

Ming took out her phone she wanted to text Kimoni.

"Hey baby having fun here but loving, missing and needing you! Out @the club smooches xoxo"

"Whew" Angie said as she walked up and sat next Ming.

"Damn girl, you startled me," Ming said to Angie.

"Sorry girl I needed to come take a break and get a drink, Nayla ass is wild and outta control down there."

"Hey she's trying to make up for closet time" Ming chuckled.

"Don't you mean lost time" Angie said looking puzzled?

"No, closet time. Her ass was never lost just locked up." The two friends both begin to laugh.

"What's so funny" Nayla asked as she walked up and grabbed her drink?

"You professed Angie we laughing at you, how you getting it in tonight aren't you?"

"Yep sure am! I need another damn drink," just as Nayla was looking around to find a pleasure girl Me'Lisa walked up with a glass of champagne.

"Excuse me this is for you," she said to Nayla handing her the glass.

"It is she asked looking surprised, who is this from?"

"The lady over there," Me'Lisa advised as she pointed to the far corner of the VIP area.

Turning to see who and where Nayla raised the glass and lipped "thank you."

The kind stranger nodded her head in approval.

"A secret admirer" teased Ming.

"Hell, I'm not surprised said Angie with the show she's been putting on, down on the dance floor!"

"Girl what are you talking about?" "I'm just dancing." Nayla said as she took a sip of the champagne.

"Right dancing," Angie repeated while looking at Ming.

"Whatever" said Nayla as she walked over to the balcony. "Hey you guys" as she motioned for both Ming and Angie to come to her. "You can see the stage from here."

"Yeah, but I'm going to be down there front and center," Angie pointed towards the stage. "I need to see everything up close on The King!"

"Knowing your crazy ass, you just might try and get on stage with her" Ming joked to Angie.

"Umm, I sure won't pass up the chance! Oh wee looking at my watch it's almost time for the show and it's a few femmes in the lineup whose ass I want to rub and drop a few ones on," laughed Angie.

"Both y'all are crazy" confessed Ming. "I'm just here for moral support."

"Yes cause you all boo'd up and shit now! So you just look and leave the touching to us," said Angie as she pointed to Nayla and herself.

"Yes hunnti, leave the touching to us" Nayla cosigned.

"Excuse me ladies," Me'Lisa said interrupting the friends chat. "The show is set to begin and the first performer will be out soon. You guys can go down and take your seats."

"Thank you Me'Lisa," said Ming. "By the way you have a very unique name, it's beautiful."

"Thank you so much and you're welcome also, enjoy the show" Me'Lisa said before she walked away.

"Ok let's hit it ladies, Angie advised as she started walking to leave the VIP area. "This is what we came for!"

"Ok I'm ready, lead the way" chimed Ming.

"You guys go ahead I'll meet you down stairs. I want thank that generous fine stranger for my drink," revealed Nayla.

"Ok see you down stairs," Ming said as she and Angie continued to leave out of VIP.

With the glass in her hand Nayla walked slow and seductively over to where the stranger was sitting to tell her thank you. "Hi" she said as she got close to the stranger. "I just wanted to come over and personally thank you for sending me this glass of champagne."

"You're welcome beautiful we've been admiring you since you walked in."

"Really," Nayla looked surprised. "Now who all is we?"

"My girl and I," the stranger said turning and pointing. "This is my girlfriend Lynn and I'm Traci."

"Hello Lynn, I'm sorry I didn't see you sitting there, thank you as well for the champagne and thank you again Traci. Well I better be getting down stairs to get my seat for the show," Nayla said.

"Why don't you join us right here" Lynn suggested while patting the sit next to her.

"Yes," Traci agreed. "Join us for another glass of champagne and tell us a little about yourself perhaps your name."

"Oh, I'm sorry my name is," Nayla thought to herself she didn't want to give her real name so she gave her middle name that also happen to be Lynn. "Lynn also, isn't that a funny coincidence?"

"Yes, it is," said Lynn as she poured more champagne in Nayla's glass.

"See that's even more reason for you to stay and have another drink with us," added Traci. "You can see the show from here."

"Sure, I guess it wouldn't hurt" Nayla gave in and agreed.

"Not unless you want it too," teased Lynn.

"Now really what kind of hurt are speaking of" inquired Nayla?

"I would love to rub and spank your pretty ass for starters," said Lynn.

"And I would like to watch if that's ok" asked Traci?

"Oh do you now, so I take it you guys like to add spice to your relationship? So why me and what makes you think I'm that kind of woman?"

"Well, Lynn and I are in an open relationship, we trust one another and we play together," Traci said as she took a sip from her glass.

"What we thought was, you are a beautiful, sexy, confident, and super fuckable woman!" Lynn added as she grabbed Nayla by the hand and led her to the seat next to her.

"Well, we are straight, forward aren't we?" Nayla said to Lynn.

"No, straight forward is saying let me eat your pussy because I want to know what you taste like!" replied Lynn.

"Umm now don't go saying things unless you really mean it. Because giving you a taste maybe something I'm willing to do," Nayla answered back.

"Ooh I like that!" "Baby did you hear that?" Lynn turned and said to Traci.

"Yes baby I did."

"Well since you are willing to let me taste it, why don't you first let me touch it Lynn" asked Nayla? Lynn moved her chair closer to Nayla and placed her hand on her thigh. "Your girlfriend isn't going to mind me touching you, will she?" Lynn asked as she moved her hand slowly up Nayla's thigh and closer to her pussy.

"I don't have a girlfriend" replied Nayla.

"Good so I can play with your pussy any way I like?" Lynn inquired as her finger tips made contact with Nayla's pussy lips.

"Oh baby" Lynn turned to Traci "you were right she doesn't have any panties on."

"Told you babe" Traci responded.

"How could you tell, do you have x-ray vision?" Nayla teased Traci.

"No baby but the way that ass was moving when you were dancing I knew it wasn't confined to any underwear," admitted Traci.

"So tell me babe is her girl shaved like you like it," Traci asked Lynn?

"Let me see" Lynn said as she rubbed her fingers over Nayla's pussy. "Yes baby and she's getting wet for me, let me see just how wet she can get."

Lynn then started to gently rub Nayla's clit between her fingers. Slowly she rubbed creating a moist thickness that told her Nayla was enjoying it.

"Umm you are wetting my fingers nice and good" Lynn told Nayla.

"You wanted to touch so use your fingers" Nayla instructed Lynn as she opened her legs wider to give Lynn better access to her love hole.

Traci set back in awe watching the show unfold in front of her, she loved to see her woman play with another woman. It turned her on and it didn't matter if she was watching or joining.

Taking advantage of Nayla opening her legs Lynn massaged Nayla's clit between her thumb and first finger creating a nice silky wetness. She then inserted her middle finger inside Nayla's pussy. Up and down round and round her fingers went playing in Nayla's paradise.

Tossing her head back Nayla being to feel the liquor and just enjoyed her pussy being played with as it was feeling so damn good.

Seeing how much both the ladies were enjoying each other, "hey how about we take this party to a private room so we all can get comfortable" Traci suggested.

"Yes baby sounds good to me" agreed Lynn as she thrust her fingers deeper inside Nayla's pussy that made Nayla purr.

"Oh, oh they have private rooms here or do we need to go get a room," Nayla asked?

"We have a private lounge room here that we can go to" said Traci.

"We can play right here at the club come on I'll lead the way if you would like" Lynn asked Nayla?

"Sure, lets' go, show me the way" Nayla insisted.

Lynn took her hands out of Nayla's pussy so that they could get up and make their way to the lounge. Dripping with Nayla's wetness Lynn put her fingers in her mouth so that she could taste Nayla's juices. While her fingers were in her mouth Lynn rolled her tongue around them savoring the taste that she was enjoying.

"Oh baby her pussy taste so sweet," said Lynn as she put her fingers towards Traci mouth to give her a brief sample of what was left on her finger tips. "Come on sweet pussy let's go play" Lynn directed to Nayla.

Taking Lynn by her free hand and Nayla in the other Traci helped the ladies from their chairs. She led the way as the ladies followed out of VIP and up another set of stairs and down the hall. Traci stopped at a door that appeared to be that of an office, but when she opened Nayla saw it was just the opposite.

It was a dimly lit room with a plush sectional couch that was huge. There was a fish tank built into the wall that had a multicolor of fish swimming aimlessly. Mirrors covered the ceiling with a bar on one side of the room and a king size canopy bed sat in the back of the room.

Lynn took Nayla by the hand and they walked over to the couch. Nayla sat down first leaning back on the couch and opened her legs slightly. Lynn followed her lead and sat down beside her she rubbed her hand up Nayla's thigh and to the familiar spot she just left. Just making sure you're still wet for me she leaned in and whispered in Nayla's ear.

After playing with Nayla's love hole for a few moments Lynn stuck her fingers inside to feel the warmth and tingle of her pussy. As she gently took her fingers out Nayla let out a purr. Once fully out Lynn put her fingers in her mouth to taste Nayla's nectar. Feeling herself getting wet, Lynn wanted their juices to explore one another.

"Lay back and put your leg up on the couch" Lynn instructed Nayla. Doing as she was commanded Nayla positioned herself on an angle. Lynn stood up and raised up her dress over her head exposing her mocha chocolate skin tone body with erected nipples that displayed diamond nipple rings. She then lifted Nayla's skirt up, that revealed her perfectly waxed pussy. *It looks and smelled so fucking good,* Lynn thought.

Lynn angled her body on top of Nayla to form the perfect scissors. Slowly she lower her body so that their pussies would be on top of each other. Lynn began to rub her dripping wet pussy on top of Nayla's creating a friction and a fragrance of ecstasy that filled the room.

Back and forth in a slow steady motion their pussies rubbed together getting to know each, exchanging one another's wetness. Closing her eyes to just enjoy the pleasure her body was receiving Nayla was lost in what she thought was a dream and didn't want to be awaken.

Sitting back watching from across the room Traci was enjoying every minute of this sexual act her girl was participating in!

Lynn put her hand under Nayla's shirt and began to rub and pinch her nipples. This made Nayla pussy get wetter which caused slurping sound every time Lynn rode her pussy back and forth. Slow sensual thrusts were the movements their bodies made as their pussies rubbed together.

Nayla's body tingled for she hadn't felt this feeling in a very long time. Words can't describe what it feels like when a woman rubs her pussy on yours making it wetter and wetter with every stroke.

Lynn tossed her head back as she began to bounce gently up and down on Nayla's woman hood. Nayla reached up and grabbed hold to Lynn's ass and helped her bounce by lifting her up and down.

"Oh, you like that" Lynn asked?

"Yes," responded Nayla as she bites her bottom lip.

Bringing her leg around to get into a cradle position Lynn laid on top of Nayla and put her breast in her mouth. Nayla licked around her nipples gently tugging on her piercing while rubbing her breast with her hands. Lynn enjoyed all the attention her titties where getting, she then begin to rub her pussy on Nayla like she was trying to enter in her. Taking her hands from Lynn breast Nayla began to rub on Lynn's ass, grabbing it bringing it closer to her as if she was able to put her clit inside her.

Looking over at her woman who was readily enjoying the show, Lynn leaned back on her elbows so that both of their pussies could be exposed along the sweet juices they were creating so Traci could get a better view.

Licking her lips longing for a taste "sit up and get on top" Traci directed Nayla. "I want you to fuck her like your clit is a dick and make my baby cum and cum hard" Traci commanded.

Doing as she was told Nayla sat up and mounted Lynn and aggressively started to ride her pussy. Back and forth her hips did a rhythm that had Lynn moaning and Traci under a trance. Rubbing Nayla's breast as she fucked her pussy Lynn was ready to cum! But she held it because the friction from Nayla's pussy rubbing against hers felt so damn good!

How good it felt to fuck another woman solely with your body, to be in control and bringing her to organism, it was powerful and exhilarating! With every thrust Nayla was ready to cum and so was Lynn.

"Oh, oh" Lynn let out soft moans.

"Ah, yes, oh," purred Nayla as she rolled her pelvic harder rubbing her wet silky pussy all around Lynn's. And with one last hard pump they both began to cream in ecstasy!

"Umm, umm" was all Nayla could say.

"I'm cuming oh my pussy baby," Lynn screamed!

Traci then walked up to the couch knelled down and began to lick both Nayla and Lynn's pussy. Taking turns putting each one in her mouth to swallow their sweet juices!

******

After calling and texting Nayla to no avail Ming gave up. S*he must be having a better time than wanting to see the show,* Ming thought. She then just turned her attention to The King's show! She was fascinated and couldn't believe her eyes, *damn what a show,* she thought!

Still exhausted from her night of passion Nayla made her way back from the club to the to her hotel room, it was past dawn and the sun was shining bright. She jumped straight in bed and tried to fall asleep recalling her night's events. But just as she was getting ready to drift into a deep sleep she heard knocking on the door and the hotel room door open.

"Hey Nayla you in here, are you decent, is anyone with you?" Was the series of question's Ming blurted out as she walked in the room.

"What," Nayla answered half way coherent.

"Get up girl chimed Angie or are you just getting in?"

"Just getting in I had a long chit chat with Ms. Champagne and now I'm trying to get some rest but y'all trout's won't let me!"

"Where, no, what in the world happened to you," Ming asked?

"Yeah, you missed one hell of a show!" "The King did her thang, added Angie.

"Girl I was having my own show but if you guys let me get a least a couple of hours of sleep I'll let you know all about it."

"Spare me the details" Ming said as she rolled her eyes.

"Girl I want to know everything lick by lick, grind by grind" said Angie.

"I just bet you do, nasty ass," replied Ming to Angie. "Ok we are leaving, don't forget tonight is the fashion show and we are surprising Rachael."

"Ok, ok now get out and let me sleep," Nayla said as she put her pillow over her head.

Angie and Ming left out of Nayla's room and took the elevator to the lobby. They hadn't decided if they would get something to eat at the hotel restaurant or go out and find an offsite place. They just decided to take a cab and find something and do a little more sightseeing.

As they walked out the hotel Angie's phone cell phone begin to ring. "Who the hell is calling my phone this early" she said out loud.

"Yeah, who is it?" Ming mocked her while laughing.

"Girl it's Rachael," just as Angie was getting ready to answer it Ming stopped her. "Don't answer she pleaded, she knows we are here but not that we will be at the show. We can't talk to or see her until tonight!"

"Ok" said Angie as she let the call go to voicemail. "I don't see why we can't talk to her now."

"So she won't ask us to come and she will be surprised when she does see us."

"Ok I guess operation avoid Rachael is in effect until tonight." Angie said in a mocking tone. The two friends then started to laugh.

Not having the time to wonder why her friends were not answering the phone, Rachael needed to get herself ready for tonight. She planned to look her absolute best for DC tonight! She just had to her to win DC over and make her one of her RL's. Time was running out as it was taking much longer than normal to convert DC, so it looked like she would have to resort to drastic measures of fucking DC before DC gave up some money. This was her #1 rule never to break but it just may have to be broken. Now the flight to NY and the hotel room was a start but, those were not things that Rachael could hold in her hand nothing to reminisce about. "Tonight, she thought it would have to be tonight." Just as Rachael was about to come up with a way to get DC up to her hotel room there was a knock at the door.

"Yes," who is it she called out?

"Room service," the voice on the other side of the door answered.

"Oh I'm sorry Rachael said as she walked to the door and opened it, you have the wrong room I didn't order room service."

"I did," DC said as she stepped in front of the door way.

"DC what are you doing here" Rachael squealed?

"I came here to have breakfast with you before I started my day DC said as she pushed the breakfast cart into the hotel room. I'm going to be pretty busy and I wanted you to be the first person I spent time with today."

"Oh, ok well you caught me by surprise let me go and freshen myself up and…"

"No DC interrupted, you look beautiful as you are now come on sit down and let's eat."

Doing as DC asked Rachael walked over and took a seat at the table while DC served her the food from the cart.

"Smells good Rachael said what did you order and how did you know what I would like?"

"Well I didn't, so I got us a variety and you can choose." After putting all the food on the table DC sat down and said grace

"So are you ready for tonight," Rachael asked DC?

"I should be asking you that DC countered, I'm always ready this is my job."

"Why would you have to ask me if I'm ready" Rachael inquired?

"Why tonight is on a whole other level, and it's going to be fast pace with lots of lights, camera, and action and you are going to have to be able to hold your own."

"Well that's not problem Ms. Carter I'm looking forward to being there and seeing you work."

"Good, glad to hear it" DC responded

After eating and exchanging more small talk DC left so that she could finish preparing for tonight. DC showed up at Rachael's room unannounced for a reason, she wanted to catch Rachael off guard to see her in her natural state and not made up. DC could tell that Rachael was a little uncomfortable so she decided to leave sooner.

DC coming to her room catching her off guard without her make up through Rachael for a loop, she wasn't comfortable sitting in DC's company plain without her face on. Even though DC complimented her throughout their breakfast she was totally out of her element. She definitely needed to be flawless tonight no question!

CHAPTER 12

The day flew by and it was time to go and show their support for their friend Rachael. Ming was ready to see some high fashion outfits, where Angie just wanted to be amongst the elite, and Nayla was still on A high from her night of adventure less than 24 hours ago.

"How do I look, Angie asked Ming?

"Radiant and flawless"

"Thanks boss lady, you look like the picture of perfection yourself!"

"Why thank you sweets, now let's go see if that damn Nayla is ready, her ass just might still be sleep."

Just as Ming said when her and Angie made it to Nayla's room she was still sleep. Ming has just used the key card and her and Angie went in.

"Get your ass up" Angie said as she hit Nayla on her feet as she walked pass the king size bed

"Umm what, Nayla uttered in a sleepy voice what time is it?" She asked barely able to open her eyes.

"Time for you to get up and get ready" commanded Ming. "How long is it going to take you to get your clothes on" she asked?

"Umm I'm still sleep, Nayla answered, I don't know and I'm tired from last night." "Can I just meet you guys?" "Leave my ticket and I'll be there later, let me get myself together."

"Your ticket is here on the TV and the location is listed just catch a cab" Ming said as she and Angie walked out.

"Chat with you in a minute" Angie said before they closed the door.

"Ok" Nayla responded as she rotated her body under the covers

"Her ass ain't coming," Angie said as she and Ming got into the cab and drove off.

NYC was buzzing with an electrifying energy. As the ladies made their way to the venue, their excitement level grew tremendously. As they got closer they could see a crowd building, the streets had been cut off and cars rerouted to accommodate the night's event. Only certain marked limos could get passed the blocked off streets to allow for the elite to make an entrance and walk into the venue.

"Hey, for the hell of it let's stand outside and see who pulls up" Angie said to Ming as the cab pulled over to let them out.

"Ok let's hurry and see who we can see," Ming answered back.

As the ladies made their way closer they could see and hear hundreds of people cheering and screaming. The energy was awesome as they walked up. The ladies stood behind the barricade separating the red carpet from the entrance.

"This is so exciting," bellowed Angie.

"Yes, it really is," agreed Ming.

"This fashion show has some heavy hitters attending" Angie observed. Just as she was about to say something to Ming a limo pulled up and the door opened.

"Oh my GOD, yelled Ming look" Angie she said!

Just as Angie was turning around to see what Ming was yelling about, out stepped DC. The crowd started to roar and the cameras started clicking. The crowd begin chatting we love you DC!

DC then turned around and helped her companion out of the limo. Rachael was the picture of perfection! Her makeup was flawless and she looked like a porcelain doll so delicate and exotic. As Rachael fully emerged from the limo the paparazzi went mad, they start yelling who is that, what's her name? Not uttering a word but smiling from ear to ear while holding on to DC tight they walked in perfect stride together.

"Damn you see that bitch!" "Our bitch said Angie that mutherfuker looked fantastic!"

"Yes, she does agreed Ming and you see that look in her eye, this is the life she wants. Her ass is not letting DC go after getting a taste of this!"

"You right boss lady she sure won't, and not without a fight" Angie agreed

"Let's go in and get our seats," Ming suggested and the two friends made their way inside. The décor inside was speculator and beautiful. The show was set to start shortly and people were mingling and making their way inside.

As Ming and Angie wondered around to find their seat they saw DC and Rachael talking to someone, as they got closer DC noticed them and signaled for them to wait a minute. DC excused herself and Rachael from the conversation they were having and asked Rachael to walk with her for a minute. As they walked DC motioned for Ming and Angie to come closer behind Rachael.

"So, Rachael remember when I told you that I had a big surprise for you today DC said. Well I need for you to close your eyes so I can give it to you."

"Oh, DC really Rachael got all excited and anxious, you shouldn't have" she said.

"Ok keep your eyes closed and turn around," just as she turned around up walked Ming and Angie.

"Ok" DC said as she walked around and stood behind Ming and Angie, "open your eyes now Rachael."

As Rachael opened her eyes DC yelled, "surprise look who's here with you La'Ming and Ms. Angie!"

With a look of confusion on her face Rachael stood in her spot without uttering a word. "Surprise" Ming said as she and Angie walked up and hugged her to snap her out her trance. "Put a smile on your face and say something Ming whispered in Rachael's ear."

Snapping out of her shock that her surprise was only Angie and Ming and not an expensive gift, Rachael tried to pull herself together and act like she was happy.

Both Angie and Ming tried to make the awkwardness of the situation better by saying "hey girl we're here it's time to party!"

"Oh thank you, thank you, for bringing my best friends to your show" Rachael said as she walked up to DC to give her a hug and show her gratitude.

"You don't look happy," DC said to her.

"No sweetie, I was just in shock! I couldn't believe that Ming and Angie were my surprise and here with me." Rachael needed to hurry up, clean up her reaction, and do some heavy damage control. Hell, she wasn't lying about what she said, she was shocked and couldn't believe that she wasn't getting diamonds but got Ming and Angie ass instead!

"Ok well, will you ladies excuse me I have to get back stage and get ready. I'll see you guys after the show" DC then gave Rachael a kiss on the check and walked away.

As DC walked away and was out of sight Ming turned to Rachael and said "what the fuck was that?" "What's wrong with you?"

Trying to pretend like she didn't know what Ming was talking about Rachael shrugged it off and replied with "what do you mean what"?

"Girl don't try to act like you don't know Angie added! The look on your face when you saw us wasn't a look of happiness or excitement."

"Yeah, Ming interrupted you looked confused and upset like you were expecting something else."

"You know she was, Angie said sarcastically with her materialistic ass, she was expecting an extravagant gift and not us."

"Whatever" Rachael said defending herself.

"Well is that what it is," Ming asked? "Because it was written all over your face and we all could see you were more disappointed than surprised or happy."

"Ming I don't wanna talk about this let's go take our seats we can talk about it later."

"Tuh, there might not be a later, DC did not look thrilled, you better walk light" Angie advised.

Not really knowing what to make of the situation Rachael just shrugged it off. She never had to work this hard to do anything when it came to a RL. "You guys I have this under control don't worry DC is fine. I just wasn't expecting y'all, but enough of this let's go get our seats so we can see my woman do her thang!"

"I agree with going to get our sets but her being your woman umm, you are delusional" Angie said as she walked away.

"This isn't the place or the time for this, Ming said. "Let's go." The three friends found where they were sitting, sat down and waited for the show to start. Within a matter of minutes the Emcee took the mic and the show was on!

The models looked great and the clothes were awesome, every time DC took to the run way there were cheers and applause. But she was professional and perfect never cracking a smile.

Smiling from ear to ear Rachael was in awe watching DC come out looking so damn and being so damn great at her job. Once the show was over it was off to the after party.

DC had instructed Rachael to take the limo and that she would meet them at the after party. She told Rachael she would call her on her cell once she made it there and that her and her friends names were on list as her guests. Rachael was not happy about not walking in on DC's arm to the after party, she told Ming and Angie they both were invited and to come on, the limo was waiting.

"Where's DC" they asked?

"She's meeting us there" Rachael advised.

Angie laughed under her breath.

As the ladies got into the limo Rachael instructed the driver where to go, she then she turned and asked "where is Nayla?"

"Girl probably still at the hotel sleep let me try and call her cell."

"No that's ok, Rachael stopped Ming let her sleep through this wonderful night."

"Honey she had a wonderful night last night chimed Angie that's why she's sleep."

They all begin to laugh.

"I don't even" Rachael started.

"Want to know" Ming finished.

"But I do" Angie added.

After arriving at the location, the ladies went in and begin to mingle they were all rubbing shoulders with some heavy hitters, just enjoying the atmosphere and having a great time.

DC arrived quietly and found Rachael chatting with her friends.

"Hello beautiful ladies", she greeted them, "do you mind if I take your friend for a moment" she asked?

"No not at all," Ming replied

"Don't just take her keep her" said Angie.

DC began to laugh, "you are quite hilarious, Ms. Angie."

"I try, I do try," Angie said.

"Shall we," DC said to Rachael as she held out her arm for Rachael to take it.

Grabbing on to DC's arm Rachael and DC walked away.

DC and Rachael mingled with the party guest and were having a good time. They made small talk, joked, ate hors d'oeuvres and had a few glasses of champagne.

Feeling the effects of the champagne Rachael told DC she wanted to get some air. The two then walked out onto the terrace to take in some of the New York air.

"It's breath taking out here and this view is beautiful," said Rachael.

"Yes, it is DC agreed, so tell me how did you like the fashion show and are enjoying yourself" she asked?

"Why yes it was wonderful, you were great, the people, this party is spectacular, all these famous people this is the life!"

"The life," DC looked puzzled?

"Yes" exclaim Rachael "your life is fantastic and it's wonderful to have all this at your fingertips, I want it! Here you've been taking me on those frugal dates when we could have been living this life together, the life of luxury!"

"Excuse me," DC said! "Did I just hear you say what I think you said? What frugal dates? Because I didn't spend my money on your materialistic ass! Now you're here and

170

you see just a piece of what this life is like and you automatically think it's luxurious? This isn't just glitz and glam, it's hard work, sweat and pain. And sometimes you get this, a little bit of a reward for your hard work, and you think you deserve to just be here just because? I thought you were different, no I thought I could show you the world isn't always about the things you can buy with money, but the things that money can't buy are more precious. But time and time again you've shown me that all you care about is money. You know what I made a mistake asking you here I should have never ever tried to pursue you. I saw the kind of person you were from the jump but I tried to show you the simple things. I see very clearly that you aren't a person who would ever be able to appreciate the simple things in life! Good-bye Rachael you can stay and enjoy this glamour-filled life that you desire so hard to have I'm done!" DC walked off the terrace down the hall and headed out the party.

Ming and Angie watched from a far what looked like a heated confrontation between DC and Rachael.

When DC walked off and left Rachael Ming and Angie went to make sure she was all right. Visibly shaking and upset Rachael stood in shock as she watched DC walk away and Ming and Angie walk up. All she could say was "I got to get out of here, get me out of here!"

DC grabbed her bag from the limo that she put there and hailed a cab. "To the airport," she instructed the driver she then called Kimoni.

"Hey man Kimoni answered how is the party how was the show," she asked?

"A disaster replied DC, Kimoni man I'm in no mood to tell you the details I just need the first flight back to Chicago asap I'm on my way to the airport right now!"

"Ok man, let me get on it and I'll call you right back."

"Ok" DC said and hung up from Kimoni, looking down at her phone she saw she had a message. She wasn't in the mood to talk not to anyone.

Kimoni came through and luckily for DC there was a flight leaving in an hour, she would be home in a few hours.

By the time, DC had landed in Chicago and was making her way home, it was almost 4am and she was plain exhausted. As she paid for the fare for the cab and grabbed her bag she noticed a car double parked in front of her building as she made her way inside she saw a familiar face.

"Tameko, DC said, True what are you doing here?"

A startled True turned around as she was surprised to hear her name being called and the last person she thought she would be running into was DC. "Hey what are you doing here True replied back?"

"I live here remember, DC said my condo is upstairs."

"Oh yeah, I know, but you are supposed to be in New York and not here. Oh, my I look a mess, you weren't supposed to see me like this way. I True stumbled over her words I was dropping off a gift for you while I had the nerve to do it." True stepped to the side to reveal a beautiful box sitting on the counter in front of the night doorman.

"A gift for me why, a puzzled DC asked, and why are you bringing it so early in the morning?" "Why don't you get your gift and come on upstairs with me."

"Oh, I just left the gym and I'm a mess plus I'm double parked," True tried to explain.

"That's nothing that can't be fixed, DC turned to Jack please park her car in my guest spot. True give Jack your keys, now that takes care of your car. Now come on up and have an early morning drink. I need to relax and I can tell you why I'm home."

Doing as DC asked True gave the doorman her keys and followed DC to the elevator. Once in her apartment DC let out a large sigh. "Damn I'm glad to be home." DC walked into her bedroom and dropped her bag she called True in as she continued to her bathroom to turn on her shower. "So,

True, what's in the box and why did you buy me a gift it's not my birthday?"

"Well I just wanted you to know that I think you are special and kind, with such a big heart and if no one ever told you, I just wanted to tell you. But here open it for yourself True handed DC the box."

Inside was a gold link necklace with a key pendant attached and a card with the words that read.

Your soul is the only one who has the key to my heart....

To be continued...